SPLENDINI!

SCOTT PINZON

Zondervan Publishing House
of The Zondervan Corporation
Grand Rapids, Michigan

Splendini!
© 1982 by Scott Pinzon
First printing, September 1982

Library of Congress Cataloging in Publication Data

Pinzon, Scott.
  Splendini!
  Summary: Fourteen-year-old Dave Scott, who dreams of being known
as the great Splendini, uses his Christian principles and a little magic to foil
a gang of international criminals trying to steal the ultimate weapon.
  [1. Mystery and detective stories. 2. Christian life—Fiction.
3. Magic tricks—Fiction] I. Title.

PZ7.P6353Sp 1982   [Fic]   82-11003
ISBN 0-310-45601-0

Illustrated by Louise Bauer
Designed by Kim Koning
Edited by Judith E. Markham

Printed in the United States of America

Contents

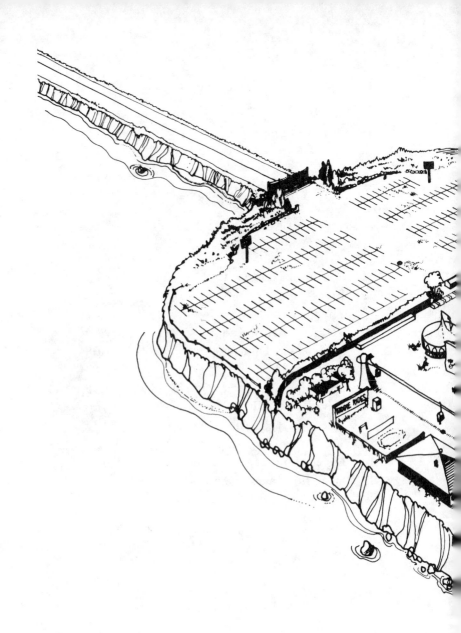

PACIFIC
OCEAN
PARADISE

Splendini Loses Control

As usual, The Great Splendini had the audience gobbling it whole and begging for seconds.

Majestic in his black top hat and tails, basking in the white-hot spotlight, he waited for the thunderous applause to fade. Just before the clapping ceased, he continued addressing the multitude. His enunciation and timing were perfect, of course. In the dream, Splendini was always perfect.

"Try as you might, you will not pierce my secrets," his amplified voice echoed through the theater. "For Splendini is the *master of magic!*"

On the word "magic," Splendini raised one gloved hand over his head. Immediately brass chords sprang full-blown from the orchestra pit. A two-foot square table floated in from the darkness, trailing a purple silk cover that caressed the floor. Splendini turned to receive the floating table, and it glided to a stop, hovering directly in front of him. Upon the table rested a golden box covered with scrollwork. The musicians settled down to serious work, filling in time.

Splendini raised the lid and tilted the box toward the audience. To them, the black interior appeared empty. He closed the lid, turned the box toward himself, moved one finger in a circle over it, then reached inside. As the golden lid glinted in the stage lights, Splendini pulled out a live rabbit.

The audience murmured. To their delight, the rabbit kicked against Splendini's chest and almost escaped, but his skilled hands kept the animal captive. He then placed it back inside the box and closed the lid.

Now Splendini closed his eyes, placed his index fingers together and held them to his chin. He appeared to be summoning unseen powers. For long moments he stood motionless.

The audience held its breath.

Suddenly, with startling energy, Splendini threw his arms wide, shouted a mystic word, and opened his eyes. Rapidly he plucked the lid off the box, holding it with the palms of his hands at diagonal corners. The lid spun in his hands, flashing gold and black and gold past the audience's eyes. He laid the panel upon the floating table and began dismantling the entire box at great speed, a panel at a time, spinning each piece so the audience could see both sides before he set it aside. Finally, all that remained was the front panel facing the audience.

Splendini placed his hand upon the panel and paused. The music pulled to a halt and idled with a roll from the timpani.

Then in one glamorous burst, Splendini threw the panel into the air and whipped the purple cover off the floating table, which in turn crashed to the stage. The rabbit had vanished!

The audience's cry mingled with a blast from the orchestra. Once again tumultuous applause filled the vast theater. Splendini bowed from the waist, holding the panel which, of course, he had neatly caught.

"Thank you!" his voice boomed over the din. "Thank you!"

When he smiled, his boyish grin revealed that for one so skilled, he was surprisingly young. . . .

"Thank you very—" The doorbell cut through his daydream. Suddenly he was no longer Splendini; he was Dave Scott, standing in his cluttered bedroom, practicing the most expensive magic trick he had ever bought. The top hat and tails became a blue Dodger baseball cap, a short-sleeved pullover with a surfer decal, and faded Levi's.

"Best in the world," Dave mumbled, and laughed at the conceit of his own daydream. World's best magician at thirteen years old? Fat chance, when he had to save his allowance for five months just to buy one illusion! He could hear it now: "For my next trick . . . I would like to repeat my previous trick."

Dave gazed ruefully at the golden box on his dresser. And fat chance at being best when the thought of performing in front of a crowd petrifies me.

A voice floated through the closed door. "Hi, Mrs. Scott. These are for you. From our garden. Amazo the Amazing Amateur in?"

He heard his mother's laugh. "What beautiful roses! Thank you, A. J.! Yes, Dave's practicing, so knock before you go in!"

Dave grinned. A. J.'s normal enthusiastic entrance could register on the Richter scale; getting him to knock would be a pretty good magic trick in itself. Quickly Dave lifted the lid of the golden box and checked to make sure the lid's nearly invisible pouch concealed the collapsible rabbit. He closed the lid and started to sit on the chair near his desk to pull on his tennis shoes when he caught his reflection in the dresser mirror.

Dave groaned. Anyone else would see brown eyes, dark curly hair pushing out from under the baseball cap, and slightly oversized but even teeth set in full lips. Dave saw four other things instead. Four neon, glow-in-the-dark, Rudolphthe-Reindeer-red, each-one-the-size-of-your-head blemishes. He knew pimples were inevitable, but did he have to be the first on his block to own some? Oh, well, they were just another evidence of his new batch of troubles. Sighing, he sat down and pulled on his right tennis shoe.

The bedroom door burst open. "Hey, Dave, look at my new T-shirt!"

Concealing a smile, Dave surveyed his tall blond friend whose chest read, "BE ALERT! The world needs more lerts!"

At the lack of reaction, A. J. lost his smile. "What's wrong? Don't you like it?"

"The door, A. J.," Dave said. "You didn't knock on the door."

A. J. slapped his forehead with one palm, as though punishing his head for letting him down. "Oh, man, I'm sorry. I forgot you were doing your magic—here, just a minute." He stepped out of the room and disappeared behind the door. After a moment, a feeble knock sounded.

"Sorry, lerts only," Dave called.

A. J. bounced into the room. "That better? You like the shirt?"

"I doubt you'll stand still long enough for anyone to read it," Dave joked. "I like it. What's in your hand?"

"Frisbee. For later," A. J. said, flopping onto Dave's bed. He flipped the black disc onto the pillow, then lay on his back and directed his long legs up a nearby wall. "And *Sports Illustrated.* I just picked it up on the way over here and I can't wait to look at it." With that, he opened the magazine, and within seconds his conscious presence had left the room.

"Have a seat, A. J. Make yourself at home," Dave said. He shook his head and bent to finish tying his shoes. Lately, even when he was at home, Dave didn't always feel at home. A. J., though, could probably feel relaxed at a Gray Panthers meeting.

After a few seconds, A. J. managed to mumble, "Huh? You say something, Dave?"

"Yeah. I said, don't get too involved with that magazine; they'll be here any second."

As Dave had hoped, A. J. looked sideways and asked, *"Who'll* be here?"

"Steve and Renee. They're picking us up today because mom has a voice student coming for a lesson right now."

"Nuts!" A. J. closed the magazine and swung his feet to the floor. "The day camp at church is all right, but I hoped we'd be late enough to miss the Bible study part for once."

Dave said cautiously, "I don't think the Bible studies are so bad."

A. J. idly thumbed through the magazine. "Steve's boring. I just endure his talks so I can hit all the hot spots afterwards."

Dave decided to change the subject. Something inside made him want to cover up; to not let A. J. know that Steve's Bible talks had hit him hard and deep. "Want to know where we're going today?"

A. J. glanced up sharply from his magazine. "Do you know?"

"Sure."

"I thought no one was supposed to know. Everyone's been guessing all week!"

"Have you heard me guessing?"

A. J. paused to think. "No!"

Dave stood up and polished his fingernails on his shirt in artificial pride. "I've got connections, you know. *Big* connections at the *top*. I'm a very busy man, very busy—"

"I know, I know, what with your world-wide magic tours and all. I've heard all that. Tell me where we're going."

Dave grinned. "We're going to tour Compudat. My dad got us in."

"You're kidding!" A. J. sat open-mouthed. "You're serious?" Dave nodded. "Wow! I've wondered about that place for years!" A. J. lobbed the Frisbee to Dave. "This is Ground to Frisbee Control. Do you read me, Frisbee?"

Dave caught the plastic saucer behind his back. "You've got the general idea. They make satellites, they do laser research, they build advanced weaponry and other stuff."

"Yeah, it's the 'other stuff' that's got me curious!" A. J. exclaimed. "On the evening news they said that foreign governments would pay millions to see some of the blueprints filed there!"

"There's a building there called 'the secret building,'" Dave said. "And everybody knows that nobody knows what's in there. But I've seen most of the plant. You'll love it! It's like stepping into the future!"

"I knew your dad had been with Compudat for a while, but he must carry some weight to get thirty kids into the plant," A. J. marveled aloud.

Dave shrugged. "Come on, A. J., he's just my dad. He just goes to work like any other dad." Then he continued in a quieter tone. "But remember last month when he was gone for three weeks? He wasn't allowed to tell us where he was going until he got back!"

A. J. let out a low whistle. "So where did he go?"

"Well—there's no harm in telling you now that he's back. Among other places, the Pentagon. And White Sands Nuclear Test Center." Then, as an afterthought, Dave mused aloud, "He's seemed a lot quieter since then." He tossed the Frisbee back to A. J., who seemed lost in thought. A. J. absently caught the disc without even glancing at it.

Before the conversation could continue, a double toot sounded from out in the street. "They're here!" Dave said. "Let's go!"

A. J. clutched the Frisbee and his *Sports Illustrated* and scooted out the door. Dave ran down the hall and poked his head into the den, where his mother was selecting sheet music by the piano for her morning teaching session. "Bye, Mom! Gotta run!" he called.

The dark-haired woman looked up and her smile reached to her brown eyes. "See ya, Magic Man!" she teased. As Dave disappeared, her voice trailed him down the hall. "Don't forget your lunch!" Dave detoured into the kitchen, snatched a brown bag off the tiled counter, and zoomed for the front door.

Outside, the radiance of the southern California morning dazzled his eyes. He trotted to the curb where A. J. had already squeezed into the back seat of Steve's blue hatchback sedan. Dave could smell the neighbor's fresh-cut lawn and hear the echo of kids down the street calling to each other from their bicycles. The day seemed full of excitement and promise. The passenger door was open, and Renee was leaning forward as far as she could; Dave tried not to crush her as he shoved his way into the back seat beside A. J.

"Good morning!" Steve said to Dave's reflection in the rear view mirror as the car pulled away from the curb. A miniature pair of track shoes dangled from the rear view mirror, reminding Dave of Steve's track scholarship to a nearby college. Steve's blond hair tossed in the wind. Despite the early hour, the sunshine allowed them to drive with the windows rolled down.

"Are we really going to Compudat?" A. J. asked before Dave could open his mouth.

"Uh-oh! Sounds like the secret is out!" Renee said. She turned in her seat to look at Dave. The college girl's straight auburn hair blew into her face, and she pushed it behind her ears as she asked with a smile, "Got any ideas who told?"

"He just found out a couple of minutes ago!" Dave insisted.

"No big deal," Steve said. "We just wanted to avoid stirring up any controversy or excitement. Looks like we'll make it without any uproar."

"I don't get it," A. J. said. "Mr. Scott wouldn't show us anything *that* secret, would he?"

"Of course not," Steve said. "But a lot of people feel Compudat is so important that no one should be admitted but employees. Costa del Mar's a small town, and Compudat is its only claim to fame."

"Whaddaya mean?" A. J. protested. "We have a pretty good go-cart track, with loads of video games!"

The others laughed. "I apologize," Steve joked. "But that's supposed to be another dark secret we were covering up." As they cornered, Steve asked Dave, "So what other secrets have you told A. J.?"

Instantly the laughter drained out of Dave. He knew what Steve hinted at. "Nothing," Dave said, trying to sound as cheery as before. In his own ears, his voice seemed to echo from a tomb. "Nothing at all." Dave stole a glance at A. J. The whole thing had passed right by him; he was paging through his magazine again.

Dave noticed his own palms sweating. It wasn't just the thought of telling A. J. about his new relationship with God. It was the possibility of losing his friend on top of everything else.

As the others continued a playful conversation, Dave lapsed into silence, staring out the window. What was happening to him? Two months ago he had no worries; seventh grade ended with him, A. J., and their friends planning to rule the school next year. But in two months he had grown two inches, and now his body moved as though he had borrowed it from someone else and it had turned out to be the wrong size. His arms and legs had organized into a rebellious army. Then the red *things* began to appear on his face. And even his voice began to betray him. Now he sounded like a combination of Mickey Mouse and Tony the Tiger. And even more embarrassing, the change could happen without warning—sometimes in the middle of a word.

And why did all this have to happen just as he became aware of girls? He had never noticed girls before; after all, one mud-pie maker was just like another. But now some of the former mud-pie makers wore make-up and looked at him with a certain look he could neither understand nor return.

This is a yucky state to be in, Dave decided for the hundredth time. No wonder they gave it a name like "puberty." The very word sounds gross. No wonder I'm afraid of people right now. I'm sort of afraid of myself.

And he couldn't talk to his best friend about it. A. J. hadn't even experienced the symptoms yet. A. J. would probably stay a kid longer than Peter Pan. He and A. J. differed as a solemn ceremonial procession differed from a circus parade, but they had been best friends since second grade. And Dave knew how A. J. felt about "religion."

He thinks it's just for girls, or skinny bookworms, or—or people who aren't quite at home with real life, Dave thought. He hates those glowy paintings of Jesus where it looks like He's wearing lipstick. I felt the same way, too, no matter what mom and dad tried to tell me, until I realized last week what it all really means. But I don't know how to explain it to A. J. He's just going to think I've turned into a freak.

Dave stared out the window, seeing nothing, chewing the inside of his lip. He felt a slight bump on one cheek. Maybe I am turning into a freak, he thought. I feel like I'm losing the real me. And I can't lose my best friend, too. I can't—

"Planet Earth to Dave Scott. Repeating. Come in, Dave Scott."

"Huh? Oh, sorry, Steve, I was thinking."

A. J. offered, "Dave thinks the real world is a nice place to visit, but he never wants to live there."

Dave gave his friend a playful punch on the shoulder. "That's because I find you waiting in the real world too much of the time. What did you want, Steve?"

The car pulled to a halt at a stoplight. Steve turned in his seat to look at Dave directly. "A. J. was just telling me that your magic's getting pretty good, but you never get to perform anywhere. I wondered if next Friday you'd like to put on a small show for the day camp. Nothing big—just thirty minutes or so. I'm sure everyone would enjoy it."

A. J. butted in with, "Speaking as Splendini's agent, my client accepts. Right, Splendini? This is our big break!"

Dave looked from A. J. to Steve to Renee, and all of them looked back at him in expectancy. To his horror, he heard his traitorous mouth lie, "Sure! Might even be fun!"

The signal turned green. Steve turned back to the wheel and drove on. "Great, Dave! We'll count on it!"

Dave thought quietly, *I'm going to die.* He shot a glare at A. J., who caught the look and in turn looked puzzled. *The idiot really thinks he just* helped *me.*

He visualized a news headline for next Friday's papers: MAGICIAN DIES OF NERVOUSNESS. Then, glancing at A. J., Dave added the subhead, "Murders Friend First!"

He didn't relax until Steve's Bible study, half an hour later. Sitting on the carpet and on folding chairs in one of the church's classrooms, nearly thirty twelve-to-fourteen-year-olds listened as Steve explained a passage of the Bible to them. He made them laugh, and he made them think; and Dave realized more each day that the Bible wasn't just a boring adult rule book. It was more like a love-letter from God.

Last week Steve had explained God's love and how the natural response was to give your love back to Him. Afterward, without understanding it all, Dave had prayed with Steve, alone, and offered his life to Jesus. When he had finished, it was all he could do to keep from crying just from the happiness of being friends with God.

But that was a week ago, Dave thought as the study drew to a close today. I know I did the right thing, but I'm not sure how to keep doing it. How do I act now? How do I relate to God?

He stole a glance at A. J., who was reading *Sports Illustrated* and ignoring the study completely. Dave felt cut off from his friend, both because of the weird changes his body was taking and because of his new attitude toward God. If only I could explain it to him, Dave thought. But I don't even know how to try.

Steve closed the study with a prayer. Then he looked up and said, "All right. I have to make a quick run to the store to pick up more soft drinks since we have some new people today. A. J., do you still have that Frisbee?"

A. J., hidden behind Barry, one of the members of next year's football team, looked up from his magazine and said, "Sure!"

"Okay. I'll just be a few minutes, so why don't you toss it around in the parking lot until we leave. Just stay away from the cars. Or, those of you who would rather sing can join Renee on the grass." The meeting broke up with a clattering of folding chairs and a jostling of knees and elbows.

Before A. J. had jogged ten feet into the parking lot, other kids called to him to throw the Frisbee as they spread across the asphalt. Renee, with two girls named Sandi and Laurie who never seemed to leave her side, and Timmy, the youngest boy in the day camp, went to sit on a small grassy patch surrounded by a brick planter. Dave saw some of the new kids he didn't know sit on the planter, not really joining either group. One slender, red-headed girl sat off by herself, looking curiously depressed.

"All right, hot dogs!" A. J. hollered. "Let's keep this thing moving!" With that he blistered the disc at Mike, a dark-headed boy who already had a fair start on a mustache even before entering ninth grade. Mike had played basketball with Dave and A. J. plenty of times after school, so he was ready for

Splendini!

A. J.'s move. He snagged the flyer effortlessly and sailed it high into the air toward the furthest corner of the parking lot.

Barry scrambled to meet the Frisbee yards ahead of him and made the catch. He flipped the disc straight toward the asphalt at an angle that bounced it up and straight toward Dave.

"Way to go!" A. J. enthused as Dave displayed his one-fingered catch. "Come on, you guys! Trick shots only!"

For the next several minutes, the Frisbee whizzed its way from leaping catches to banked throws to bounce shots and backward throws; from a high-rising, slow-dropping glide to a burning beeline. Lisa, the pastor's daughter, topped them all with a carefully slanted fling that went up, out, around the top of a lamp pole in the parking lot, and gently into the hands of a stationary A. J. At that, the group broke into cheers.

"That's nothing!" A. J. bragged. "Watch this! It'll come right back to me!" He doubled up, then hurled the saucer into the wind as hard as he could, nearly straight up. The black Frisbee flashed up to the lamp pole, but instead of going around, it smashed into the light. A metallic *spang!* rang out, and the entire aluminum assembly wobbled. The disc veered crazily, then headed straight for the planter where the visitors sat.

"Look out!" shouted A. J., both hands to his head. The red-headed girl, with her back to the game, looked up just as the Frisbee rushed for her face. She only had time to let out a squeal and throw up one hand before the plastic disc smacked her between the eyes. Her glasses flew through the air and tumbled into the grass.

"Oh, my gosh!" A. J. exclaimed. He ran for the girl, calling, "Are you all right?"

Dave ran for the girl, too; in fact, all the Frisbee-players did. She had both hands to her face and sat doubled over the planter as if in agony. At first Dave thought she was bleeding, but then he realized she was trying to hide the fact that she was crying.

A. J. reached her first. "Are you all right?" He placed his hand gently on her back and stooped, trying to see her face.

"Leave me alone!" the girl demanded, her voice strained with anger. She glared up at A. J. for a moment. Braces flashed in the sunlight as she ordered, "Just leave me alone!" Then she buried her face in her hands again and let out a muffled sob.

"I'm really sorry," A. J. said. "I didn't do it on purpose."

The girl gave no sign that she heard him. All they could see was wavy red hair hiding her face as her back shook silently.

By this time all the kids had gathered around. In the awkward silence, no one knew what to do. Renee said, "Sylvia, are you injured?" The girl wouldn't answer.

A. J. picked her glasses out of the grass and rubbed them on his T-shirt, trying to clean them off but mostly succeeding in smearing them. Then he crouched near her again and said, "Here's your glasses. They aren't broken or anything."

The girl exploded. "Why can't you leave me alone? Go away, all of you! Stop staring at me like some attraction in a zoo!" She tried to cover her face with one hand while she waved everyone away with the other. Dave saw tears tracing lines through her freckles. Too astounded to move, everyone did the opposite of what she had just ordered.

"I said *leave me alone!*" she shrieked, and she hurled herself at A. J., thin arms flailing at his chest. Her impact knocked him from his crouching position onto his back in the grass.

"Hey now!" A. J. shouted. "Knock it off!" For a few seconds he tried to capture her wrists, but she kept swinging wildly. Finally he had no choice. He gave her a strong shove that sent her staggering backward; then he leaped to his feet.

"I'm not your punching bag!" he declared. "I've already apologized to you, and it's obvious you aren't hurt! Now lay off or I'll give you what you deserve!" In disgust he tossed her glasses at her feet, whirled, and pushed his way out of the circle.

The girl scooped up her glasses and ran the opposite direction, back toward the classrooms.

Suddenly Steve's voice asked, "What's going on here?" Unnoticed, he had returned.

Renee said, "A. J. can tell you. I'd better go after Sylvia." Then she turned and hurried toward the building.

"Everyone into the bus!" Steve said. "We're leaving in five minutes! Let's go!"

The kids began to file onto the old yellow bus. As Barry passed, Steve handed him a grocery bag full of canned colas and instructed him to put them in the ice chest already on the bus. Then Steve signaled A. J. to join him a little distance from the line of kids.

Dave recognized the look on A. J.'s face. It usually appeared only when a teacher told him to stop talking out of turn or called him up to the front desk for not turning in homework. Dave tagged along.

"It looks pretty bad for you, A. J.," Steve said in a low voice after the kids had passed. "I saw you shove Sylvia and yell at her. What happened?"

"I didn't do anything wrong!" A. J. blasted back.

"Keep your voice down," Steve urged quietly. "No reason to include the whole group in this thing. You're not in trouble—yet. Why did you push Sylvia?"

"She started it," A. J. said sullenly. He stared at the ground and kicked at a grease spot.

"We were playing Frisbee, like you said to," Dave offered. "A. J. tried a trick shot and accidentally hit Sylvia, but not that hard. He went over to apologize, and she just started yelling at him and pounding on him!"

Steve frowned. "That doesn't make sense. Isn't there more to the story? Why would anyone act like that?"

"Because she's *weird*," A. J. stated.

"She really did act strange, Steve," Dave persisted. "I've never seen her before. Who is she?"

"She's new in town. That's why I feel so bad that this happened. Let's wait a minute; here she comes now."

The boys did not turn around to look. A. J. kept his hands in his back pockets and kicked stubbornly at the ground with one foot. Dave stared at the side of the bus. As they approached, Renee said something to Sylvia, and without looking up, Sylvia headed for the bus while Renee crossed over to join Steve and the boys.

"Did you see what happened?" Steve asked.

Renee sighed. "I guess I did. A. J. accidentally hit her with his Frisbee, but she wouldn't accept his apology and flew into a rage when he gave her glasses back. I assumed there must be more between them, but she says she's never seen A. J. before. That true, A. J.?"

"You bet," A. J. said. "And she doesn't have to ever see me again, either. Tell her to feel free to leave."

"So why did she get so mad?" Dave asked.

"She wouldn't tell me much," Renee said. "She just tried to stop crying." She paused in thought for a moment. "The bump from the Frisbee may have set her off, but I think she's really upset about something else. During the worst of her crying, she kept repeating, 'I can't fail father. I can't fail father.' When I tried to find out what she meant, she wouldn't say another word. Steve, do you suppose her father died recently or something?"

"I don't know, Renee," Steve shrugged. "I've only had one conversation with her; just enough to know that she's new in town."

"There's something definitely wrong," Renee said. "A thirteen-year-old girl doesn't act like that over a slight embarrassment. But I think it's going to be a while before she feels comfortable enough around us to tell us more."

"Okay," Steve said, then sighed. "I guess we'll have to leave it at that. Whatever the case, you still shouldn't have pushed her, A. J. You're too strong. Since you couldn't make up with her, just stay completely away from her until you both feel better. Got it?"

To Dave, it seemed Steve was blaming A. J. for what had happened. He started to defend his friend, then changed his mind. He had already done all A. J.'s talking for him; he should let his friend speak for himself.

But A. J. didn't answer Steve. He looked up for the first time in the whole conversation and said, "Can we go now?"

"Go ahead."

Dave and A. J. headed for the bus. Under his breath, A. J. murmured, "Let's sit together. I want to talk to you."

Dave nodded. He was worried. At this rate, he was afraid A. J. might not come back to church again.

Noisy chatter filled the bus as Dave and A. J. boarded and looked around for a double seat. With all the new kids, just about every seat was taken. In the back, though, Dave could see two empty seats separated by a couple of people. Maybe one of the kids would move over with the other and open a double seat for him and A. J. He led the way to the back.

As Dave came within three seats of the back, he gave an inward groan. One of the two people was Sylvia. Not much use talking to her; maybe the other girl would move.

"Shelly," Dave asked the blond-haired girl with braids, "A. J. and I need to sit together. Do you think you could move over by Sylvia?"

Shelly glanced apprehensively at Sylvia, who was sitting there remote and detached. She gestured for Dave to move closer. Dave bent down and put his ear by her mouth so she could whisper.

"I don't mind," Shelly breathed, "but I'm afraid of her. If

she says it's okay with her, I'll move. You ask her."

Dave grunted assent and stood upright. He faced Sylvia and cleared his throat. "Sylvia." She didn't respond. "Sylvia, would it be all right if Shelly sits next to you?"

Sylvia sat still for so long that Dave almost started to ask again when she turned her head and glared at him. She seemed to have ice in her eyes. Dave felt adrenalin pump into his gut.

"I saw you gossiping about me, both outside and just now," she pronounced crisply. "I think your attitude is totally reprehensible. And as for your friend—" She paused to coat A. J. with frost from her eyes. "He's done more damage than he knows. I suggest you both leave me alone, or you may find yourselves in horrible trouble. Unexpectedly." She turned her head and stared out the window. "Sit elsewhere."

Dave gaped. "You're *threatening* us?"

"Wow, listen to Miss Vocabulary," A. J. mocked. "What are you gonna do? Talk us to death?"

Sylvia gave her attention to them once more. "I'm not talking about what *I'm* going to do, but you wouldn't understand that. Nor would I expect cretins and imbeciles to understand an adult vocabulary. Allow me to translate." She packed an amazing amount of force into two words: "Get lost!"

Something in her tone began to unlock all the frustrations Dave had felt for the last few weeks. He found it hard to control his anger; after all, this skinny creep was threatening his friend . . . and him.

"Now look," he began, "you're the visitor here. You can't just boss us around and insult us. And just because you use big words doesn't mean you can threaten us! If you hate us that much, do us all a big favor and just get out of here!"

"What makes you think I want to be here?"

"What makes *you* think we're gonna let you *stay* here?" A. J. said. He pushed past Dave and grabbed Sylvia by both shoulders. He pulled her to her feet and shoved her into the aisle. "Get out of here, crybaby!" A. J. blustered.

Sylvia reared back and swung at A. J., intending a good hard slap. This time A. J. was ready and easily avoided the blow. Instead, her palm caught Dave on the cheek.

Dave saw red. He clenched his fist and threw his arm back to punch her. But a powerful hand gripped his wrist like iron and Steve's voice said coolly, "Renee will sit with Sylvia. We have two more seats up front."

In his anger, Dave hadn't heard Steve's approach. Now the hate drained out of him and he suddenly felt stupid. Punching out a girl half his strength! He could still see the fleeting glimpse of panic that had crossed her face as she saw him start to slug her. His face burned with embarrassment.

"Saliva started it!" A. J. accused. He pushed past Steve and stormed up the aisle.

Dave hung his head. He couldn't lift his eyes from the floor. "Sorry," he mumbled.

"This isn't like you, Dave. What's the matter with you?"

Dave couldn't answer. He slid past Steve and trailed A. J. toward the front, his thoughts buzzing with fury inside his blue baseball cap.

Jerk, he thought. Nerd. How will you ever tell A. J. about God now?

Void of energy, he flopped into the seat next to A. J. "Forget about our talk," his friend said. "There's nothing left to say."

What do I do? Dave wondered, staring at the metallic seat back in front of him. I hate her. I know she's got problems, but it's not fair. He tried to get a grip on his thoughts. No, that's not right, I shouldn't hate her. I know I shouldn't, but I can't help it, I *do*—

Where was all of that love God promised when he needed it? He was trying hard to be something he couldn't be, do something he couldn't do. Once again he pictured the fright on

Sylvia's face when she saw his punch coming, and he died a death of shame.

Some magician I am, he thought. Things would be so much easier if I could just make her vanish.

He couldn't know that he would get his wish sooner than he thought. But Sylvia wouldn't be the only one to vanish.

2 # Break-In

"Wow!" A. J. exclaimed. "Look at the size of that thing!"

"Keep moving," Dave said, pushing him from behind. "You're blocking the doorway."

A. J. stepped to one side of the huge double doors that opened into Compudat's lobby, but he kept his eyes on the two-story-tall globe that dominated the lofty room. Sequential lights twinkled all over the globe, indicating the paths of orbiting satellites Compudat had built. The huge sphere nestled in a four-foot-high planter filled with draping ivy, and the sheen of the leaves changed colors with the blinking lights. Plush couches surrounded the planter. To one side of the room, a break-away model of the lunar landing module squatted in a glass case; to the other side, information and reception counters ran the length of the wall and ended near three elevators. Above the counters hung the Compudat trademark, with electrons and protons orbiting a globe that formed the "o" in Compudat. As the kids filed in, they automatically hushed their voices and threw their heads back to look for the ceiling three stories above.

Even Dave, despite many trips to Compudat, still marveled at the technological achievements symbolized by the Compudat globe. Some of his tension dwindled in the atmosphere of the bright lights, the luxuriant surroundings, and the excitement of the moment.

"What's that on the wall?" A. J. asked, nudging him. "Are those real photographs?"

"Callisto, one of Jupiter's moons," he said absently, watching Sylvia file into the waiting area, Renee close behind. With a heavy sigh, he added, "Sent back by Voyager II."

"What's so sad about—" A. J. broke off, following Dave's gaze. "Man, don't let her bother you. I almost forgot the whole thing already."

"I can't help wondering about her comment," Dave said "'I can't fail father.' And she cried so hard—"

"She's just a weirdo," A. J. said. "Case solved. Are we meeting your dad soon?"

"Yeah, I think he'll be coming out of those elevators." "Come on." They threaded their way through the crowded lobby.

A soft rumble came from behind one of the elevator doors as the boys approached. Then the door whisked open and two men, one slightly plump and balding and the other tall with curly brown hair, stepped into the lobby. The plump man wore a knee-length white smock, but the taller, younger man sported a flashy shirt, open at the throat, with gold chains surrounding his neck. From a heavily jeweled right hand drooped a smoldering cigarette.

"Excuse me," Dave said. "I'm looking for Dean Scott, the senior systems specialist here. Do you know him?"

The plump bald man smiled and the flashy dresser let out a chuckle. "I've only been here three weeks, and I know Dean

Scott. Everyone here does. You must be his son." The flashy dresser moved the cigarette to his left hand and offered the right to Dave in a firm handshake. "Warren Michaels. Plainclothes security. Since I'm still a little new around here, I'm taking the tour with your group today. Glad to have you here." His smile revealed nicotine-stained teeth.

"I'm David Scott. And this is my friend, Alexis Jerome."

"A. J.," amended his friend. "People don't usually have time to say 'Alexis Jerome' when I'm around."

Michaels let out a booming guffaw. "A talker, huh? Well, we've got something in common, A. J. I like your shirt, too."

"I'm Howard Ludlum," the white-coated man said. "And let me say, I have immense respect for your father, David. His reputation is well-earned."

"Why, thanks," Dave said. He had the impression that this man didn't throw compliments around lightly. "Do you know where dad is?"

Across the lobby, a set of automatic doors slid aside and another man strode briskly into the room, carrying a clipboard. Although white streaks peppered his hair, he had a young, rugged appearance about his wiry frame. His dark mustache turned up at the corners as he smiled in recognition of Dave and A. J. hurrying toward him.

"Hi, boys," he said. "Looks like you brought a pretty big group with you!"

"Over thirty, dad," Dave said. "You'd better make this good or I'm in big trouble!"

"Nothing to it," his father said. "I see you've already met Howard and Warren."

Steve and Renee had been talking to the receptionist behind the counter. Now they made their way through the crowded lobby to Mr. Scott. "Thanks for getting us in, Dean," Steve said as they shook hands. "The kids will never forget this, I'm sure."

"My pleasure, Steve. I believe in your ministry. In fact, you've done so much for Dave—"

"I think we'd better get started now," David broke in nervously.

"Dave's right," Steve said. "But I do appreciate your taking the time for us. I'm sure you're very busy."

A tired look passed over Dean Scott's face. "This month, I'm always too busy. There's a stack of urgent papers waiting on my desk right now, but they've been there for days, so— what's three more hours?" He brightened. "Gather the kids and follow me through this corridor. We'll officially start the tour in the heat-test chamber. Ready, Howard? Warren?"

The scientist and the rent-a-cop nodded agreement and followed Scott up to the automatic doors he had just come through. Steve called for the attention of the kids, who had spread through the lobby, and told them to line up.

The day-camp group jammed the entryway of the corridor leading into the heart of Compudat. Soon the boom of many voices echoed in the hallway, carrying over the amplified sound of feet on tiled floors.

Dave and A. J., just ahead of the group, found themselves the captive audience of Warren Michaels, who had taken it upon himself to fill Dean Scott in on his past accomplishments. At first, Michael's stories seemed lively and humorous, but after several minutes Dave noticed a pattern. All the stories ended with Michaels as the smartest or the quickest, and famous people seemed constantly to be asking his advice. Finally, Dave turned his attention to the space shuttle pictures on the walls, and he noticed A. J. doing a poor job of concealing a yawn.

The other kids, however, seemed dazzled by Compudat. They gawked at the close-circuit television cameras that hung from the ceilings and pivoted to follow the group. They puzzled at the long, technical titles on the doors of offices they passed.

After a few minutes, they had turned so many corridors and crossed so many intersecting hallways that everyone felt lost.

"I get it," A. J. said finally, interrupting Michaels, who had remained as talkative as Howard Ludlum was quiet. "We're all supposed to be white rats, and your dad wants to see how long we take to find our way out of here, right?"

"Well," Dave replied, "speaking strictly on your behalf, there is a definite resemblance." He ducked as A. J. tried to knock his cap off his head.

The group came to a checkpoint where each person had to remove the contents of his or her pockets and step through a metal detector. Then they proceeded down one more hall past an intersecting corridor. The other corridor opened onto an immense indoor construction area, where they glimpsed a five-story rocket gantry and several men working with forklifts. Then, without fanfare, they found themselves crowding into a room lined with computers.

"Please step to the back," Scott told the first few kids who entered the room. "We'll have to crowd in tightly to fit." Steve urged the group into place as Dean Scott and Howard Ludlum turned their attention to the wall of computers.

Dave was squished into the back corner with A. J., Barry, and Timmy. Barry pointed to the back wall, inches away, covered with electrical wires as numerous as noodles on a plate of spaghetti. "What's all this, Dave?" he asked. "With all these holes and wires, it looks like an old-fashioned telephone switchboard."

"Don't bother asking," A. J. said. "Dave just told me he's never seen the heat-test before."

"I haven't. But I can tell you what that is. It's a patch bay."

"The electro-mechanical wonder strikes again," A. J. mumbled. "You must get it from your dad."

"No, I just read a lot of books."

"What's a patch bay?" Timmy piped.

"The wires lead somewhere else, probably to the computers. They can unplug one end of the wire and connect it to another lead out, changing the function of the wire. Maybe they want the computer to measure temperature this time, so they plug a wire in here; but maybe next time they want to measure voltage, so they plug a wire in over here. I'm guessing a lot, but that's the general idea."

"So what happens if I take two of 'em and stick 'em in Sylvia's ears?" A. J. asked. Barry tried not to laugh.

"What happens is a Compudat security guard kills you," Dave warned. "This stuff is delicate and expensive!"

"Just kidding! Just kidding!"

As the last person crowded into the room, Warren Michaels closed the door. Ludlum now sat at a console that looked like an electric typewriter with a television screen suspended over it. As he began to type, green letters and numbers filled the screen. Beside him, magnetic tape reels on the wall automatically spun and halted, started and stopped. A hum accompanied the colored display of lights that shifted back and forth across banks of control panels.

Dean Scott hit a switch and the lights in the room went out, except for small working lights near the computer terminal where Ludlum sat. For the first time, Dave noticed at the other end of the room a door with a small window in it and several LED meters shining with crimson numbers. A light shone through the window in the door.

"Welcome to our temperature test chamber," his father began, "and welcome to Compudat. I think you noticed our hallways here are slightly larger than in your homes." The group gave an appreciative murmur.

"I can't tell you everything Compudat does," he continued, his hair shining with red highlights from the LED meters, "because we have a key role in advancing our national security. However, we also attempt to move ahead in many scientific fields, including space flight. That's where this room enters the picture.

"In the small adjoining room behind me, we can lower the temperature to four hundred degrees below zero; or, we can heat it to over twelve hundred degrees. That's like the freezing vacuum of space and the friction of reentry into Earth's atmosphere. Many of the circuits that go into a spacecraft have to handle both extremes, so this is where we test them."

Dave stood on tiptoe to see over the heads of those directly in front of him.

"I can't see," Timmy whispered.

"We're ready now for a heat test on some silicone chips. These are electronic circuits like you find in a common pocket calculator, and they've all been wired to the computer." He consulted his clipboard, then said, "These particular circuits must withstand nine hundred degrees of heat. That's twice the temperature at which paper bursts into flame."

Lisa raised her hand timidly, then asked, "Is there any danger of a fire in here?"

Scott smiled. "Not really. The heat-chamber walls are made of concrete blocks. This experiment is done many times a day and has never gone wrong at this particular facility. However, should a fire break out, the entire plant is honeycombed with alarms that ring when a flame is in the area. That way, we know which way to run—away from the alarm!" Some of the group giggled nervously. "Before we start, are there any other questions?"

Hands went up all over, and he began to call on them, one at a time.

"Why did you turn the lights down?" Shelly asked.

"It makes it easier for us to read the LED displays behind me. This one gives the temperature in the next room; the others indicate stress, weight, density, and other conditions of the circuit we're testing."

"I can't see anything," Timmy whispered again.

"No problem," A. J. whispered back. "I'll lift you up on my shoulders."

"Maybe I should do it," Barry offered softly. "I'm stronger than you."

"Who says?" A. J. squatted. "Climb up on my shoulders, Timmy."

"Be quiet, you guys," Dave said.

Sandi, standing next to Renee as always, asked, "How do you make the temperature rise?"

"Good question. Mr. Ludlum uses the computer both to raise the temperature and to check how the test chip is doing, simply by programing the machine through that keyboard where he's sitting. Why don't we go ahead and start, and you'll see what I mean. Then we can take any other questions. Howard?"

The red numbers on the wall read 76.80. As the screen in front of Ludlum flickered, the balding man caused the temperature to slowly climb. Silently, the group watched in fascination.

In the darkened back corner, Timmy had decided to try Barry's shoulders. "Move, Dave," Barry breathed. "I need some room for this."

Dave tried to push into the person in front of him. He had to turn sideways to get out of the way, and found himself looking toward the door where Warren Michaels stood.

"Wait, I'm taller than you," A. J. said. "I should do it."

"Come on!" Dave said. "Get on with it!"

The temperature had passed the two-hundred-degree mark, and still climbed steadily. Absorbed in the experiment, the group ignored the whispered undertone in the corner. Heat waves shimmered in the small window.

Something strange caught Dave's attention. Warren Michaels was glancing back and forth from Dean Scott to

Howard Ludlum, as if to see if they were watching him. Then he reached behind his back and silently turned the doorknob. With a last narrow-eyed glance at the two men, Michaels opened the door, slipped into the corridor, and closed the door behind him.

Abruptly the argument behind Dave's back escalated.

"It's okay, I've got him, I've got him," A. J. muttered.

"Look out, you can't balance like that," Barry insisted.

Dave and the people in front of him turned just as A. J. tried to stand rapidly, supporting Timmy on his shoulders. He tried to balance, but had nowhere to move his feet. Timmy's weight pulled A. J. sideways, and they crashed into the wires of the patch bay.

Frrzzap! A brilliant flash illuminated the room for a fraction of a second. A. J. and Timmy toppled to the floor and a shower of sparks burst from the board, cascading over them. One of the girls nearby let out a short, clipped scream. Timmy started to cry.

"What's going on back there?" Scott demanded. Urgency crackled in his voice. "Hold the experiment, Howard!" The LED numbers flickered and held at 502.11.

Scott hit the lights, and everyone blinked in the sudden glare.

"I'm sorry! I'm sorry!" A. J. called from the floor. "It was an accident! Timmy, are you all right?"

Timmy responded with more tears. Barry stooped and plucked him off the ground, extracting Timmy's arm from under A. J. with difficulty.

"Please let me through," Scott said. "Let me see what's happened." Nearly all the kids began talking at once as he tried to find a path through the densely packed room. With laborious progress, he struggled through the kids, who pressed against each other to move out of his way. Some of them fired questions at him.

"Don't worry!" he called. "I don't think it's anything serious, but I need a closer look. Stay calm and try to let me by."

Just as he reached the center of the room, a muffled thud shook the walls and the room went black as a tomb. The group gave a frightened cry.

"Stay calm!" Dean Scott repeated, louder. "There's no need for alarm!"

"What's going on?" someone complained. Another plaintive voice said, "I'm scared!" A confusing chorus of voices began chattering all at once. Dave could hardly tell if his eyes were opened or closed in the darkness.

"Someone open the door!" Steve called over the voices. "There may be a light outside—"

Suddenly, with a burst of color from the computer lights and a hum of machinery, the power turned on again.

"Listen to me, everyone!" Scott called, squinting in the radiance. "Apparently there's been a circuit overload. I doubt if it relates to the wires in the corner. The light we have now is from an emergency backup generator installed for just this kind of situation. We'd better leave the building until we know the precise problem. But I don't want anyone to run. Got that? There is no immediate danger, so do not run."

"But what about the heat test?" It was Sylvia's voice. "Look!"

Heads turned toward the temperature display. In the confusion, the surge of returning power had taken the temperature to nearly one thousand degrees. Howard Ludlum gasped. "Oh, my—"

The clanging of the fire alarm tore through the hum in the air. People screamed.

Suddenly a mass of bodies crushed toward the door, surging like an ocean swell.

"Don't panic!" Dean Scott yelled. But the deafening alarm outshouted his voice.

"The computer doesn't register a fire!" Ludlum cried. "There's some mistake—"

"OPEN THE DOOR!" several kids yelled.

"Back up!" Steve ordered. He fumbled with the doorknob, which somehow had been locked. Suddenly the door opened and bodies spilled into the corridor. Another alarm in the hallway screamed its alert.

"I don't know where to go!" one boy cried. "I'm lost! I'm lost in here!"

"HOLD EVERYTHING!" Steve bellowed. His voice commanded obedience. "We have to follow Mr. Scott! Now *don't run,* or you'll fall and get hurt!"

David's father fought to the door and into the corridor. "Don't run!" he repeated. "Walk stooped over, like this!" He began a brisk shuffle down the corridor, bent at the waist to avoid smoke inhalation. A semblance of sanity returned to the group as they began their escape, following the scientist and imitating his gait.

"Is Timmy all right?" Dave questioned Barry.

"He's just scared. He can walk. I'll watch him," Barry stated. Even the football star showed the strain in his voice.

"Dave," A. J. said, "tell me it's not my fault!" He looked pale, afraid.

"Don't worry," Dave said. "Let's get out of here first!" He pushed his friend toward the door.

Renee stood at the door, holding each person back until the previous one had gotten a good start down the hallway. "Go!" Dave shouted to her over the alarms. "I'll bring up the rear. I know the way!" Renee hesitated. "They need someone in the middle of the group," Dave insisted. Without a word, she nodded and hurried down the corridor.

The mob lurched along, twisting and winding through the corridors like an enormous drunken centipede. With great difficulty, the kids tried to keep from panicking and running.

Alarms sounded at almost every intersection, urging them on; but Dave, bringing up the rear, saw no smoke or flame yet. Behind him, in the direction of the construction area, he heard men's voices shouting to each other.

He rounded a corner and saw a chubby boy leaning against the wall, crying and gripping his side with one hand. "I can't go on!" he sobbed. "My side—"

"Come on!" Dave urged. He swallowed hard. He didn't like the eerie feeling of being last. With a rough shove, he forced the other boy down the corridor; the retreating backs of the others were still in sight.

As Dave scurried through the maze, he noticed the cameras staring blank, motionless, and wondered what had happened in the monitor room. Then as he crossed a familiar intersection, a sudden thought struck him. His father had mentioned important research papers on his desk. If those papers burned, months of work would go up in smoke. This was the hall leading to his father's office; the alarms were still silent here. He knew what he had to do.

The chubby boy still lagged. Dave swatted the boy's behind and shouted, "Go!" As the boy jumped forward, Dave whirled and sprinted down the intersecting hallway.

He pounded down the corridor, made a left and a right. His breath came hard as door after door flashed past. For once, he was grateful for the extra two inches in his stride. Finally he saw the door he wanted. The sign read, "Dean Scott, Senior Systems Specialist."

Grabbing the doorknob, he jerked himself to a halt. Almost out of control, he slammed into the wall, then flung the door open.

A surprised cry greeted him as his eyes photographed a thousand impressions: papers scattered over the floor, desk drawers lying upside down on the desk, file cabinets hanging open. A small bearded man glared fiercely at him, then grabbed several documents. Before Dave could move, the man spun around and vanished out the other door.

"Hey!" Dave yelled. "Hey, stop!" Quickly he scooped the nearest sheaves of papers into his father's open briefcase, slammed it shut, and turned to pursue the intruder. Suddenly, the harsh clanging of fire alarms pierced his ears again.

Unsure, startled, he looked at both doors. Outside both of them, the alarms jangled. The fire had surrounded him!

3

The Gang
of 53

Dave snatched up the briefcase and jumped through the door the intruder had used. He glanced both ways down the lengthy passage, but the man had disappeared.

Cradling the briefcase under one arm like a football, Dave ran down the corridor. At first, panic fueled his effort; no telling how much time he had lost taking the detour to his father's office.

Once, he thought he heard footsteps following him, and he figured the intruder had circled around behind him. But when he turned to check, the lengthy hallway was empty.

After he had rounded three more corners and the alarms began to fade in the distance, he slowed to a steady jog. Finally, at one intersection, he stopped to catch his breath. Something definitely did not add up. He glanced around to get his bearings, uncertain of where he could find an exit at this end of Compudat.

He sniffed the air. Not a trace of smoke.

A mosaic mural down one of the halls looked familiar, so he

headed for it, his thoughts buzzing furiously. Finally he saw the red of an EXIT sign dully reflected on the linoleum floor, and moments later he stepped into the summer sunlight.

Evacuated office employees stood in clusters on the grassy strip that surrounded the building. A couple of them glanced at him as he opened the door, but he received no further attention.

Dave still breathed heavily. He removed his baseball cap and scratched his head while he got his breath and his bearings. This part of the parking lot faces east, and dad was leading the group to the north exit. No one else will know who I am if I try to report the break-in, so I'd better just find dad. He began jogging along the side of the building.

When he got to the corner of the building, he saw, in the distance, the day-camp group standing on a large grassy island in the center of the parking lot. Most of the kids faced the building, watching an army of tan-uniformed Compudat security guards complete the evacuation.

Dave shouted, "Dad!" and waved one arm over his head. A small figure in a gray suit turned and waved back. Still carrying the briefcase, Dave trotted across the lot, threading his way through parked cars until he reached the group.

His father had turned from a conversation with Sylvia. Dave, seeing the concerned look on his father's face, had the absurd feeling that Sylvia had been tattling on him. Instead, his dad said, "Dave! Where have you been? I was worried about you!"

Dave handed the briefcase to him. "Here. I went to get your papers. I was afraid they'd burn. And—"

"Son," he interrupted, "I appreciate the thought, but you're much more valuable to me than any of my work. You could have been killed in the fire!"

"But, dad, listen to this—"

Before he could finish, Sylvia interjected, "Mr. Scott, is that the man you were looking for?"

Dave and his father turned and looked where Sylvia pointed. Howard Ludlum, exhausted, perspiration shining on his bald head, staggered toward the group and collapsed in the grass.

"Howard!" Scott rushed to Ludlum's side. "Are you all right?"

"I'm . . . fine!" The man gasped, his portly chest heaving up and down. "I just got . . . turned around—"

"Dad, this can't wait!" Dave insisted. "Someone just broke into your office and stole some papers!"

Ludlum and Sylvia let out surprised exclamations, but his father absorbed the shock in silence. Grimly, he spun a four-digit combination on the lock built into the briefcase. As he did so, he said, "Tell me the rest, Dave. What did you see?"

By this time, A. J. had made his way through the group to Dave, and he looked on with interest as Dave said, "The office was all torn up, dad. This guy had gone through your file cabinets and drawers and tossed some books off the bookshelf. He looked like Mr. Fashion, with a suit and all, but he was a little dude with a beard and—" Something triggered in Dave's memory, and he saw the frozen instant when the man had glared at him—the burning eyes, the dark blond beard and hair, and something else. "And a scar! He had a scar on his right cheek, almost all the way from his ear to his mouth. The beard hid it partly, but I remember the scar. When he saw me, he ran. I tried to chase him, but he disappeared."

His father shuffled some papers from the briefcase. "I think it's good you didn't catch him, because he would have been extremely angry at you. The most important papers are still here. Apparently you interrupted him before he finished his mission."

"I don't understand how the guy could move so fast," Dave said. "I came into the hall right after him, but he was gone. Except once I thought I heard someone behind me, but he wasn't there." A sudden thought struck him. "Mr. Ludlum, you left late, too? Did you see anyone like that in the halls?"

The scientist had gotten his breath back. Perched upright in the grass, his white smock tangled between his legs, he faintly resembled Humpty Dumpty after the fall; but the serious tone in his voice commanded careful consideration. "You said a small man with a dark blond beard and a scar?. No. I saw only Compudat employees. I know I would recall if I saw someone like that."

"I think we'd better tell security about all this." Scott rose to his feet and motioned to a guard in an electric cart, some distance across the parking lot. Then he began questioning Howard Ludlum to make sure the heat test had been shut down safely.

Renee had gathered some of the kids under the single shade tree that graced the grass island, leading them in songs, while Steve calmed the rest of the kids. The chubby boy sat on the curb, still gripping his side and swallowing hard.

A. J. threw an arm around Dave's shoulders and gave him a quick, hard squeeze. "Glad you made it, Klutzini," he said with relief. He turned to face Dean Scott, and for the first time Dave noticed the anguish on his face. With difficulty, A. J. said, "It's my fault. I know this doesn't do much good, but I'm sorry." He paused as a choking sound crept into his voice, and Dave realized his friend was struggling not to cry. "I would never have picked Timmy up if I'd known those wires could cause a fire." A. J. blinked back the threat of tears, barely winning his battle. "Mr. Scott, I can't let my dad find out—"

"But there's something I don't understand, A. J.," Scott said. "That patch bay wasn't connected to anything of importance. We don't use that kind of circuitry in modern computers. You couldn't possibly have caused a fire, yet there was one."

Suddenly the equation clicked in Dave's mind. "Dad! Can those fire alarms be set off by hand?"

"Certainly. Sometimes a technician may become aware of a fire before the alarms can detect it. In that case, there are countless places in the halls and offices where the alarms can be hand-activated."

"Then I don't think there was any fire at all, dad."

"I agree." Ludlum surprised Dave by joining in. "The computers never indicated any problems in the heat test chamber."

"I see," Scott said in a tone that said he really didn't see. Then he snapped his fingers. "Of course. With all the security guards around here, a fire alarm might be the only distraction large enough to let someone sneak into my office."

"If your theory is true," Sylvia joined in for the first time, "and there was no fire, that explains how the intruder vanished so quickly."

Dave looked at her. She had listened quietly ever since he first ran up to his dad. "You assumed he would be running for an exit, too, but if he set the alarms off himself, he would know there was no need for haste. He could've hidden in the next office."

"Sylvia has something there," Scott said. Dave and A. J. shot glances at each other. Just then, the guard pulled around in a circle and stopped his cart by the curb. "Sanders, is the fire under control yet?"

Creases in the guard's grizzled face set off the serious look in his eyes as he said in a low voice, "There was no fire, Mr. Scott."

"Then that confirms what my son suspects. He witnessed a break-in of my office. Would you please have someone check on that?"

"Immediately." The guard pulled out a walkie-talkie and extended the antenna. He spoke a few terse sentences into it, then put it away. "They're already onto it. But I'd like to take your son for further questioning."

"I have a question first," Scott said. "If there was no fire, why did all the power shut down moments before the alarms went off?"

"We found that someone had shut it down by hand in the basement," the guard said. "That's the most effective way of canceling video scrutiny. The back-up generators only power lights, air, and certain crucial computers."

Dean Scott assimilated this new theory, then seemed to put it off for closer inspection later. "My son will give you as complete a description of the man who searched my office as he can. Go with him, Dave."

Dave walked around the cart and climbed into the passenger scat.

"Then I didn't cause a fire?" A. J. said hopefully.

"No fire, son," the guard told him.

"Darn." A. J. said, trying to hide his relief. "And I was looking forward to getting my name in the paper."

"I've only read a few issues of your local paper," Sylvia said, "but from what I've seen, they wouldn't know how to spell 'A. J.'"

The guard and Scott laughed, agreeing that *The Daily Champion* definitely lacked in technical expertise. But Dave and A. J. just stared open-mouthed at Sylvia.

My gosh, she's human! Dave thought as the cart pulled away from the curb. She actually made a joke! Gee, maybe A. J. and I won't have to die after all!

Dave wondered about Sylvia's veiled threats. "In horrible trouble. Unexpectedly." She couldn't be serious! Yet, at that moment, she had been anything but playful. And he wondered about her cryptic references to her father. Was the man missing? Ill? Dead? Had he made her take a vow not to be hit in the face by Frisbees?

Or perhaps the whole thing meant nothing and wasn't worth his time. But he wasn't about to let go of it yet.

In fact, he spent enough time distracted with Sylvia's behavior that it wasn't until an hour later, as he left the security office, that another question occurred to him.

Where had Warren Michaels gone?

* * * * * * * *

That night, Dave had forgotten all his questions as he carried a small package out of the magic shop and slid into the car next to his dad. His thoughts stuck with Splendini's upcoming magic show on Friday.

"Thanks for the advance on my allowance, dad. Now I can disappear in a cloud of smoke! All I have to do is run this copper wire from the flash-pots to a power source, like a car battery or something, and—" He trailed off, noticing his father's expression, gloomy in the moonlight. "I'm sorry. I keep forgetting how boring this is if you're not into it."

His father stirred as though coming to the end of a long train of thought. He inserted the key into the ignition and started the car. "No, Dave, I wasn't bored. You know I like your magic. I'm just worried, that's all."

Dave didn't know what to say. His dad rarely seemed to worry. In fact, he usually talked about letting God handle his worries. But something had penetrated Dean Scott; something that could frighten a father.

Dave ignored a car with a weak left headlight as it pulled out of a parking lot across the street and waited to turn in their direction.

"What's wrong, dad?"

His father spun the wheel as the car turned a corner. Finally he answered, "The truth is, Dave, I don't want to alarm you. But now that you seem to be involved with my latest project—" His voice trailed off, and he showed no sign of continuing.

"What do you mean 'involved,' dad?"

With hesitation, his father said, "I'm thinking that if you saw whoever it was that searched my office, they must have seen you, too. I'm wondering what they might do about it. You have the ability to identify someone who is committing crimes on an international level."

Surprise flooded Dave. "Dad, those papers on your desk—do they have something to do with your trip to the Pentagon last month?"

His father sighed. "That's right." He seemed divided; wanting to talk and at the same time feeling compelled not to.

Dave sat and waited. This already sounded so far above his head, so strictly adult, that he didn't know how to react.

After a moment, his father continued, as though talking to himself. "Somehow, someone has found out what we're up to, and they're after the blueprints. That's all we've really got so far: talk and blueprints. I can't figure out how they moved so fast."

"But, dad," Dave cut in, "that guy only got one glance at me! He hardly saw me at all. And if he shaved his beard off, I don't even know if I could recognize him again—well, except for that scar."

His father swiveled the car through another corner and stated, "He doesn't know what you saw or didn't see. And it's obvious he wasn't working alone. He couldn't shut off the power in the basement and set off the fire alarms at the same time."

"But now that these guys tried and failed, Compudat will have its guard up, right? There's not much anyone could get away with now!"

"That's just it." Tires scrunched on asphalt as his father pulled the car to a halt at a red light. He looked at Dave. "Our guard was up. It would be impossible for me to exaggerate how secret this project is, and yet someone found out. It makes it seem useless to even try to protect ourselves. Someone in our own ranks is giving us away."

The light blinked green, and they drove on. "Dave, have they taught you in school about the Manhattan Project?"

"I read about it in a history book, dad. It was the code name during World War II for the project that developed the atom bomb."

"Exactly. And probably the most hush-hush secret ever, because of the devastating impact of the atom bomb. Not only did they code name it, but government officials almost never used the code name!" For a moment his father hesitated, almost as if he would halt the conversation. A grim look crossed his face. "It makes the atom bomb look like a water balloon, Dave. It's the ultimate weapon."

Dave's mind reeled. His mouth hung open. "How—how could anything have that much power?" His father just shook his head.

"But why us?" Dave exploded. "Dad, what kind of men do you work for? Killers? Who sits around just thinking of better ways to erase humans off the planet?"

"No, no Dave, it's not like that," his father interrupted. "Did you read that article in *Scientific American* that I gave you?"

"About particle beams?"

"Yes, and the Gang of 53. Remember them?"

"Yeah. Let's see—fifty-three scientists, physicists, and engineers who work for the Secretary of Defense at the Pentagon." It clicked. "The Pentagon—!"

"That's it, Dave. They were studying particle beams; ways to take parts of an atom and hurl them with tremendous force and focus—like man-made lightning bolts. There was no big rush; the idea was just to 'keep up with the Russkies.' But they stumbled onto something much bigger. We'd be fools not to pursue it. It's a weapon for which there is no known defense, and we dare not let it be turned on us."

Dave sat in silence, a barrage of reactions pouring through

his mind. He didn't know much about war; it seemed wrong to him, but he felt too uneducated to take a stand either way. But now, not only was the United States developing this weapon, but it might be lost and turned against them! And somehow he and his dad were caught in the middle! To think that earlier today, in an office in sleepy little Costa del Mar, he had accidentally prevented an international crime—nah, it was all too crazy.

Dave was confused. On another level, his own safety was at stake. Where does God fit into all this? How involved does He want to get? If my safety matters to Him, couldn't I just waltz through dark alleys and mine fields and leave the worrying to Him? No, that doesn't make sense; why should I have Him looking out for me in ways I can look out for myself? But then where does He come in? Do I have to wait until it's life and death before I pray?

"Needless to say," his father was saying, "none of this conversation can be repeated, son. To anyone. And we'll have to find a way to protect you. For now, stay with the group at day camp. Hopefully, no one would try anything with a crowd around. Especially not at a resort town like you're going to tomorrow. Violence would stick out like an air-raid alert."

The two rode in silence for better than a mile. Black silhouettes of shrubs and trees silently flickered past, punctuated by stark patches of white street light shining on the sidewalks and lawns of the residential street.

Then his father introduced a new subject. "I enjoyed meeting that girl Sylvia today. Is she a friend of yours?"

Dave eyed his father, trying to see if he was working up to something. "No. I just met her. Today was her first day at day camp."

"That's right, she mentioned that she's new in town. In fact, she just marched right up and introduced herself to me.

She asked very perceptive questions about the heat test, almost with the wisdom of an insider. She's certainly tuned in to science. You know, with your interest in mechanics and electronics, and her interest in applied science, I bet you two would hit it off right away!"

Now Dave knew she hadn't said anything to his father about their disagreement. "Yes, I almost hit it off with her today." He looked over to see if his dad noticed the implications.

His father was gazing intently into the rear view mirror. Dave twisted his neck and looked out the back window. Just coming around the corner, a car with a weak left headlight followed them at a distance.

"Dad—"

"I know. We're being followed."

His father made a left around a corner, then took another left so that he headed the opposite way from their original direction. "This should tell us if it's coincidence."

They inched down the dark street, his dad's eyes glued to the rear view mirror. Dave kept turning to check, his heart pounding. Just as they reached the end of the block and turned left again, a pair of headlights threw beams their way as a car turned down the street.

Without a word, his father accelerated. He turned once more, completing his circle of the block, and gunned the car straight across the intersecting street ahead. As the car jounced over the dips, the other car appeared, a block behind, and his father turned at the next right.

Streetlights sped by. His father flashed his brights at each intersection to warn oncoming traffic, instead of slowing down. They twisted toward home in the maze of residential avenues.

After several turns, his dad slowed down and stated, "I think we've lost them." He sat back in his seat more comfortably. Dave suddenly realized that he had been on the edge of his seat for the past several minutes. He hadn't seen the other car for several turns, either. He began to relax.

"Who do you think it was, dad?"

"I don't know. I wish I could've seen something besides just headlights."

As they rounded the corner a block and a half from their ranch-style home, a car squealed around another corner and roared straight for them. It was the car with the weak headlight!

"Dear God!" his father exclaimed. He jammed his foot against the accelerator pedal and swerved past the other car, which screeched to a halt and began to back around. The family wagon zoomed past their street and whipped down the next one. As they approached another turn, his father maneuvered the car into someone's driveway, killing the lights and motor and gliding to a stop fifty feet from the street. "Get down!" he ordered.

They slumped in their seats. His father's hand shot up and twisted the mirror so he could see the street while slumped down.

He had scarcely dropped his hand when the headlights whipped around the corner. A red Mustang II raced past them and took a skidding turn down another street. Father and son exchanged looks of relief, but stayed down. To move the car now would only give away their position.

The roar of another engine grew in the night. At twice the speed of the first car, a silver Porsche shot past them and hurtled around the curve.

Dave glanced at his father. Their eyes met in shared bewilderment. Two cars after them? Or someone pursuing the pursuer?

His father cracked the window open and listened. In the quiet night, Dave could hear the second car speed down the next block. He heard a double splash of shallow water as the car roared through an intersection, but soon the engine noise faded in the distance. Somewhere else, in a back yard perhaps, two cats screamed angrily at each other, startling Dave. Then the steady throbbing of crickets resumed.

"Let's go for it, dad," Dave urged. They both sat up, and his father started the car. As they shot backward out of the driveway, a light came on in the kitchen of the house where they had parked. They zoomed away, and scarcely a minute later bounced into their own driveway.

The garage door rose automatically in eerie greeting. With perfect timing, his father hit the close button before the car even entered the garage, and they slipped under the descending door.

The door drifted to the ground. From outside, no one would know a car had been by in the last few minutes. In the garage, Dave and his father sat motionless, feeling their hearts pound double-time.

"Okay, okay," Dave said. His voice chose that moment to slip into its Mickey Mouse mode, sounding tiny in the darkness. "So maybe the guy did see me."

4

Terror
at Arrowhead

To the casual observer, it would seem that Dave Scott had done nothing for the last half-hour but sit on a bench in Arrowhead Village, plagued by a coin that kept disappearing from his hands and reappearing in his nose, ear, or pocket.

To Dave, it seemed he had done much more than sun himself in the mountain air three hours north of Costa del Mar and idly practice slight-of-hand. His mind had bounced from the streets of his neighborhood at night to the counsel chambers of world powers to a laboratory very similar to Dr. Frankenstein's. Where else would someone invent the ultimate death weapon?

In order to get alone, he had sent A. J. away at the first opportunity. That must have been an hour and a half ago, and since then he had thought so intensely that he couldn't hold a single thought in mind any longer. But he could hold an emotion, and it was fear.

Yet somehow, in the warm light of day, the subdued chase

in the dark last night seemed unreal. After they got in the house, his father had immediately shut himself into his study and talked for over an hour on the telephone. When he came out, he told Dave that everything was not what it seemed; in reality, they were safe. And that was all he would say, except to add that he had probably told Dave too much already.

Come on, dad, Dave thought. I think I'm old enough to handle the truth. But whatever the truth is, I can't just hide in my room all day for who knows how long. So here I am with the day camp, and even though I'm sitting alone, I'm in full view of the counselors, like a good boy.

Dave had tried praying. He operated in a vacuum, though; it was still Steve's God, not quite Dave's God. He didn't know what to say or how to say it, which made him feel like his prayers bounced back at him off the ozone layer instead of heading for heaven. He wished he knew more about God and how to pray.

Where yesterday he had felt insecure, today he felt absolutely insignificant. How could God worry about his safety or his friendship with A. J. while He had to stop arch-villains who wanted to blow up entire countries? Every time, his thoughts circled around to the same blank wall: he needed to know more.

That's enough, Dave finally thought after he had gotten good and depressed. There's nothing one kid can do anyway, so I've got to make myself forget all this and force myself to have a nice time today. You will have fun, and you will *like* it.

A voice came from behind him. "Can Dave come out and play now?"

"Yes, his nap is over," Dave replied.

A. J. circled around to sit next to him on the bench. Like Dave, he wore a bathing suit and a colorful T-shirt, but A. J.'s shirt said, "Pobody's Nerfect."

"Sorry to send you away, A. J., but I had a lot of thinking to do."

"That's all right, Dave." A. J. gave him a look which Dave recognized as an "Is this guy okay?" look. "I don't know how you can just sit and think. I've gotta get out and shoot baskets or something, and even then I don't really *think* think; the answers just come to me. Sometimes. You all right now?"

"Sure," Dave said. Inwardly, he felt awkward; he couldn't tell A. J. about the chase last night, and he rarely kept secrets from his friend. "What's the matter with your nose?"

"What do you mean? Is there something on it?"

"Just this." Dave reached over and seemed to extract a quarter from A. J.'s nostril.

A.J. laughed. "Is that all that's left of the dollar I stuffed up there?"

"You guys are gross," someone said. The boys looked behind them and saw Holly and Denise carrying snow-cones on their way back down to the lake. They both had towels draped around their necks, and their hair had been wet.

"Oh, please, Holly, you know I can't resist flattery," A. J. begged. The girls laughed and stopped at the bench.

"I was just talking to your girl friend while we waited in line for our snow-cones," Holly teased A. J. Her short dark hair hung limply on either side of brown eyes and a turned-up nose smattered with freckles.

"Uh, yeah, my girl friend," said A. J., who didn't have a girl friend. "Which one?"

"*You* know. Your new steady, Sylvia!"

"*Sylvia?*" A. J. exploded. Holly and Denise laughed at their own joke, elbowing each other and savoring his reaction. Dave, watching the three, began to get an uneasy feeling. The laughter sounded slightly mean to him, and he knew the only humor in the joke was a backhanded insult.

"Yes," A. J. recovered, "I did ask Saliva to go steady; you're absolutely right. The only problem is—" A. J. paused for effect. "She used such big words, I couldn't understand her answer!"

Even Dave hid a smile as the others laughed at the thought of A. J. and Sylvia together.

"Here's the good part, though," Denise said. The plump girl dropped her voice to a conspiratory tone. "You know how everyone's wondered about Sylvia's father? Well, Holly was talking to her in line, and—"

"And I mentioned that the ice cream at my father's restaurant was better and cheaper than the stuff up here," Holly said. "Hold this, Denise." She handed Denise her snow-cone and began to brush her hair. "Then I asked her, real casual, 'What does your father do, Sylvia?' And we had been talking and joking and stuff, so she was kind of off-guard, and here's what she said." Holly leaned in as if revealing the location of treasure. "She said, 'I don't know exactly what he's doing now. I haven't seen him for three months.'"

A. J. whistled. "Then he probably did split—"

"Wait, that's what I thought, too," Holly said. "I told her, 'Gee, that's too bad. Sometimes I think my parents might divorce, too! And she looked all surprised and said, 'No, that's not it. That's not it at all. He's—he's—just gone away temporarily.' So I said, 'Is that what your mom says?' Then she started getting all mad the way she does, and she said, 'You cheap gossip! I'm *proud* of my father!' So we just bought our stuff and got out of there. Imagine, calling me a gossip, right to my face!"

A. J. shook his head. "If Sylvia's so proud of her father, why's he missing and why can't she say what he does?"

"Really," Denise agreed. "If she'd just admit her family is having some problems, I'd at least feel sorry for her. Instead she acts like she's just so special."

"Special, my armpit," A. J. said. "I'd like to take her down a notch or two." Then he sighed and added, "I'm sorry. I don't mean that. I just get irritated when I think of her."

"Maybe she's telling the truth," Dave said quietly.

The others looked at him in surprise.

"Yeah, you're probably right, Dave," Holly said. An edge of sarcasm crept into her voice. "Her dad is probably a hit man for the Mob, or a special assignment CIA agent, or something plausible like that. No wonder she can't tell us what he does."

"It's not as ridiculous as it sounds," Dave said. "My dad is involved with all kinds of top-secret stuff." Oops, he thought, I forgot. Shouldn't have let that slip.

"That's just it," Holly said. "We all know your dad is involved with top-secret stuff, but you don't act like you're better than us, and you don't get all mystic about it. There's something wrong with that girl."

"She's new in town," Dave said. "She might be from a part of the country that's different from California. The way everyone keeps pumping her for information, I think I'd shut up, too. Who cares what her father does? Let's give her a chance to make friends with everyone, and then maybe we'll all find out."

"If she keeps acting the way she does, she never will make a friend," A. J. said honestly.

Dave gave up. "All right, all right. But until we have more facts, it's not right to spread the idea that her father ran off and left his family." He looked pointedly at Holly. "That's all I'm saying."

"Well, well." Holly gave a smile that was close to being a sneer. "Awfully sweet on Sylvia, aren't we, David?"

Dave fought back both resentment and insecurity. He hadn't meant to defend the girl to the point of losing another friend. His ego shrank in panic, and he tried to cover with a joke. "Oh, no," he replied. "A. J. and I could never be engaged to the same girl." He smiled.

"Take this back, Holly, it's starting to drip," Denise said. She handed the sno-cone back to her friend.

"Thanks, Denise," Holly said. She slurped some liquid off the top. "After all, nobody likes drips." With a glance of indictment at Dave, Holly added, "See you around, guys," and the girls shuffled away.

"Drips?" A. J. said to Dave. "Was that meant for us?"

"Just me," Dave sighed. "That's what I get for opening my big mouth."

A gust of wind blew the sound of laughter to them.

"That's our group!" A. J. exclaimed. "We're going to miss the Water Olympics! Come on!"

Dave and A. J. leaped up and ran down the sloping village streets toward the shore. A short block later, they left the village behind and found most of the kids standing in a ragged circle on the sand near the lake. They joined the edge of the group. Steve and Renee stood in the middle of the circle wearing shorts and T-shirts.

"All right, all right," Steve was saying. "We'll see in a moment who's superior. Let me finish explaining."

The girls laughed again. An impish grin on Renee's face told Dave that something was up. He and A. J. stood on tiptoe, trying to hear and see.

"We've marked two squares in the sand," Steve continued. "Each contestant has to keep one foot in one of the squares. You can pivot on that foot, crouch, dodge, or do anything except move that one foot off the ground or out of the square. The other foot is free. You get a water balloon in each hand, and so does your opponent. The two squares are only six feet from each other, and the object of the game is quite simple: kill or be killed! Now, how shall we divide the teams?"

"Girls against boys!" called two of the girls.

"Let's go for it!"

"Snuff City!"

Splendini!

"Aw *right!*"

The noise turned into a chant: "Girls against boys! Girls against boys!"

"Okay, okay," Steve said, laughing. "I guess it's decided. Who's first?"

Renee concluded a hasty, whispered conference with Sylvia and said, "You and me, Steve!" The group cheered.

Steve smiled the smile of a cat alone with a wounded bird. "You're on!"

They took their positions in the middle of the circle, each of them standing with one foot in a small square etched into the moist sand. Barry emerged from the crowd, lugging a cardboard box full of colorful water balloons. "You may choose your weapons!" he intoned, offering the box in turn to Renee and then Steve, who each selected two balloons. "On my signal, you may fire at will." He set the box on the ground, then turned his back to it and faced Steve and Renee. In anticipation, the circle backed away from them. Meanwhile, behind Barry's back, some girls stealthily loaded up with balloons.

"FIRE!" Barry yelled. Immediately Steve hurled an orange balloon straight for Renee's brunette head. To his surprise, she pivoted backward in a complete circle, came around to face him, and blasted a red balloon into his torso. The balloon spattered against his stomach with a *paf!* and left a huge wet stain on his shirt.

Steve's mouth dropped open, and he stood wide-eyed, staring at his shirt. Before he could even look up, a green balloon burst against his blond hair. The boys groaned and the girls cheered. Steve looked up at Renee, who put on an innocent expression and shrugged her shoulders, joking, "I didn't even know it was loaded!"

In the middle of her line, he let fly his other balloon and hit her in the shoulder. The balloon bounced off and fell to the ground, where it lay quivering like a frightened jellyfish.

"No fair!" Steve cried. Then he grinned. "Okay, two points for the girls and one for the guys, because I did hit you!" The girls cheered again.

"Okay," Renee said, "A. J.'s next. Who do you want to challenge?"

A. J., in the back of the crowd, looked surprised. Renee repeated the invitation, so he pushed his way through to the center of the circle. As he took his position on one of the squares, he surveyed the circle and then said, "Gee, I don't know—"

"How about Sylvia?" Renee offered from the rear.

Dave saw a battle flicker across A. J.'s face. A. J., normally a forgiving person, finally couldn't resist such a prime opportunity. "Okay." He grinned. "Saliva."

Sylvia stepped forward, a look of complete calm on her face, and Renee handed her two water balloons. She looked A. J. up and down as if measuring him, then said, "Thank you for the chance." A. J. laughed at her as Steve handed him two water balloons.

"On my signal," Barry reminded. A. J. bent in a half-crouch, one arm cocked to throw, and turned sideways to Sylvia, giving less of a target. Sylvia stood with her feet together and her thin arms dangling straight down. Her bushy red hair and sleeveless cotten pullover made her seem painfully thin. She said, "Wait," and handed her glasses to Renee. Another girl, lugging something heavy, joined the rear of the crowd.

Dave fought within himself. He knew A. J. could throw the balloons hard enough to knock Sylvia right off her feet. Dave didn't like the girl, but for reasons unknown to him, God did. "Hey you guys," he said a little too quietly, "this isn't fair—"

"FIRE!" Barry yelled.

Water balloons bombarded A. J. from every direction,

exploding in ribbons of colored rubber and sprays of water. *"Hey!"* A. J. screamed, covering his head and shoulders with his arms. The water would have drenched him except that some of the girls missed their target. After the first volley, A. J. looked up, shook dripping strands of hair out of his eyes, and fired his balloons into the crowd. A satisfying *spush!* and a screech sounded. A. J. scrabbled for some unbroken balloons rolling on the ground, then glanced up at Sylvia. "Oh, no—"

Hefting a large bucket of muddy lake water, Sylvia drowned A. J. Large sheets of water cascaded over his back as he scrambled to turn and crawl away. "Help!" he yelled. "You guys!"

Quickly Barry and Dave grabbed for the cardboard box. Dave snatched three balloons before two girls tore the box away from him. Barry grabbed for the box but hit the edge, upending it and spilling the balloons to the ground. Some of them broke, while the mob dived for the others.

Pandemonium followed. Dave felt fingernails scratching one arm, turned and ducked just in time to avoid a flying balloon. He fired at Lisa. A tangle of flying water and grabbing hands surrounded him. Meanwhile, A. J. dished out revenge with relish, hurling water bombs as fast as he could grab them.

A rising scream carried over the racket, and Dave glimpsed Steve carrying Renee to the lake, her feet flailing. She pounded on his back until he flopped her into ten inches of water. She tried to get up and push him down. Yelling war cries, girls ran to assist Renee, and soon the whole fight had sprawled into the lake.

Within twenty minutes the initial wave of water fighting had spent itself and only the die-hards battled on. The rest of the afternoon passed rapidly into evening as most of the kids tried to devise ways of drying off, keeping to the sun as the shadows lengthened.

Later, feeling the part of the triumphant warrior, Dave ran to the church bus to get his jeans and jacket. The water fight had been exactly the release he needed. His hair had remained relatively dry because of his baseball cap, but his T-shirt clung to his body in sticky dampness. Even in summer, gathering night in the mountains brought a crisp chill with it, and he fought an occasional shiver when the wind sprang up.

He found his jacket and Levis in the back seat of the empty bus. As he pulled them on, something heavy in one jacket pocket swung against his hip. He thrust his hand into his pocket and found the flash-pot kit. With all that had happened last night, he had forgotten to take it out. He was relieved that no one had stolen it. He shoved the kit back into his pocket and bounded off the bus, looking for A. J.

Dave met Steve, coming toward the bus. He had a towel draped over the back of his neck. "Hey, partner," he greeted, "find A. J. and let's go. We told the parents we would leave at dark, and it's nearly time now. I've rounded up just about everyone else."

"I don't know where he is, Steve."

"Try the village. I think he was looking for a place to dry his hair." Steve grinned. "I hope you know that Renee wasn't picking on A. J. with that trick. She thought maybe this way A. J. and Sylvia could work off their differences."

"I guess she's trying to make Sylvia feel in on the fun," Dave said. "A. J. usually thrives on that stuff, but I'm not sure how he'll take it, coming from Sylvia." As Dave spoke, most of the church group arrived and swarmed around them, boarding the bus.

"I think he'll feel fine after that fight. He did pretty well for himself. And there wouldn't have been a joke on A. J. if he hadn't agreed to pick on Sylvia. Now hurry, he's the only one we're waiting for."

Dave ran into the village. He checked the town square and poked his head into the ice cream shop. Then he checked inside a public restroom.

Splendini!

A soft roar greeted Dave's ears as he stepped inside. A. J. was bent over beneath a hand-dryer, letting it blow on his hair. He had put Levis over his swimming trunks, too. With his head turned sideways, he caught sight of Dave and broke into a smile. "Hail, Attila the Hun. I saw you adding to your collection of heads today!"

"I hear you did all right, too," Dave answered. "Let's see how you look."

A. J. stood up and modeled for him. His straight blond hair was plastered to the sides of his head, except for his bangs, which flipped straight out from his forehead. Dave started laughing. "You look like a drowned weasel!" A. J. groaned and stuck his head back under the blower.

"They're waiting for us, A. J.," Dave urged. "Can you hurry?"

"Tell them I'll be there in a minute," A. J. grumbled.

"Look, you can wear my baseball cap to cover your hair. Here."

"Thanks," A. J. said, taking the hat. "Just let me try a minute more. Tell them I'll be right there. I wish I had a comb!"

"Okay. See you at the bus." Dave jogged out through the village to rejoin the group. Steve already had the motor running.

He hopped aboard the bus as Steve cranked the ignition, coaxing the engine to life. After a moment, the motor fired up and then idled normally. Steve frowned at the dashboard. "Running hot," he said.

"I found A. J.," Dave said, "He's drying his hair. He'll be here in just a minute."

"Okay," Steve said. He turned and called back through the bus, "Everybody sit down and strap in! We're about to leave!" Renee began seating the kids and helping them stash towels and extra clothes in the shelves running the length of the bus

64

above the seats. Soon everyone was ready and waiting.

Barry, near the driver's seat, asked after a moment, "What are we waiting for?"

"A. J.," Steve stated. "Sometimes it seems that kid is always in the wrong place at the wrong time."

"I'll go get him," Dave offered. "I won't be a minute."

Steve pulled the lever that folded the bus door open. "I'll turn the bus around while you're gone, so we'll be ready to pull right onto the road when you get back. Hurry!"

Dave ran across the dirt lot where the bus sat, kicking up dust as he ran. Instead of heading for the street, he took a shortcut behind the row of shops. As he neared the public restroom, he cut through some bushes and then stopped. Several feet away, A. J. emerged from the bathroom, wearing the baseball cap over his sun-bleached hair. Dave ducked back into the bushes, planning to jump out and startle his friend.

Dave peered through the leaves of the bushes. A. J. evidently had a rock song in mind, because as he walked he pantomimed playing an electric guitar. Dave snickered quietly. A. J. had almost stepped into position.

Suddenly a thrashing of dry leaves sounded behind A. J. He whirled around. From out of nowhere, two men wearing ski masks and dark blue turtlenecks rushed at him.

Instinctively, A. J. dodged. The slippery footing of dried pine needles and acorns caused him to fall flat on the ground, and the men struggled to a stop to grab him.

Transfixed by fear, Dave watched from his hiding place in the bushes. What could he do?

A. J. scrambled to get his feet under him and let out a yell. One of the men grabbed him from behind in a powerful bear hug and lifted him a foot off the ground. The smaller man cuffed A. J. across the cheek with an open hand and ordered, "Shut up if you know what's good for you!"

A. J. thrashed frantically, kicking and struggling, wild-eyed. The strong arms of the man hugging him crushed the air out of his lungs as the men began to carry him toward the forest. With a sudden effort, he slipped out underneath the arms and ran in Dave's direction. "Hel—"

In two bounds, the smaller man tackled him and they crashed to the ground. A. J.'s head hit a stone and he lay still.

"Slippery brat," the taller man said, his voice muffled by the ski mask.

"Let's get out of here. Someone must've heard that," Dave heard the other man say. Dave fought an overwhelming impulse to run. He had to see where they were taking A. J.

As the smaller man got up off the limp form and brushed himself off, the first man picked the boy up effortlessly and slung him over his bulky shoulder like a rolled-up carpet. A. J.'s arms dangled down behind the man, lifeless, and for a second Dave thought maybe his friend was dead.

He fought the fear down. No, that's ridiculous, he's just stunned, Dave thought. I've got to stay calm.

Moving rapidly now, the men hustled A. J. into the woods. Dave lost sight of them, but he heard their progress. Their footsteps stopped and a car door opened. Quietly, Dave stepped out from the bushes and snuck after the men. He did his best to keep silent, but each of his steps sounded to him like a herd of buffalo tromping through the forest. His heart seemed to pound even louder than his footsteps.

From behind a huge pine, he peered into the brush. He could just make out a maroon van with the back door open. The big man propped A. J. up for a minute while the other man, in short, efficient motions, slapped strips of black tape over A. J.'s eyes and mouth. They wired his wrists together behind his back, tossed him into the van, and slammed the door.

The larger man stepped around the van, out of Dave's sight. The other man took a furtive look around, as though checking to make sure they hadn't been seen.

Dave ducked back behind a tree as the man turned in his direction. He held his breath as the angry eyes behind the ski mask seemed to burn into him. A chill of stark fear washed over his body. Then he heard another door slam and the van start.

Dave wasted no time. He spun and pounded away, faster than he ever imagined he could run, back for the bus. He stumbled over pebbles in the dirt lot as he approached the idling bus. "Steve!" he heard himself scream. *"Steve!"*

Too slowly, much too slowly, Steve opened the bus door. "Where's A. J.?" He sounded cross.

"Steve—A. J.'s been kidnapped!"

Everyone on the bus stared at him. Dave realized for the first time that he had tears on his face. "I just saw two men grab him and throw him into their van! We've got to stop them!"

Steve, like everyone else, looked totally stunned. "What two men, Dave? Where are they now?"

Just then Dave saw a maroon flash among the trees that lined the road the bus faced. "Here they come!" he shouted, pointing. "You gotta believe me! Big guys wearing ski masks! A. J. tried to get away but he hit his head—"

The maroon van roared by at high speed. Dave glimpsed two men in the front. The one on the passenger side seemed to be pulling something off his head.

Dave shouted, near hysteria, "There they go! *After them!"*

★ 5 ★

Miracle and Disaster

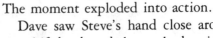

The moment exploded into action.

Dave saw Steve's hand close around the gearshift knob and throw the bus into gear. The engine roared into life, blurring all other noises, adding urgency to the confusion. They shot onto the mountain road with a jolt that would have knocked Dave off his feet, except that he caught himself on a supporting pole behind the driver's seat. Loose cola cans, swim fins, lunch bags, Bibles, and other objects tumbled off the shelves onto the camper's heads and bounced into the aisles. Renee was suddenly standing, forcing the children to sit down and buckle in. Everyone shouted questions. Ahead of them, the van disappeared around a bend in the road.

"They acted like killers!" Dave said. "I was just a few feet away! It could've been me!"

"Calm down," Steve ordered, keeping his concentration on the road. "No more of that 'killer' talk. A. J.'s still all right, isn't he?"

"He hit his head on a rock. Maybe he's just unconscious, but if you'd seen it happen—"

Steve's firm voice cut through Dave's panic. "I don't want to panic the others, Dave. And I need you to keep a clear head. You're the only witness."

Trees and rocks rushed past at blurring speed. The bus took a bend awkwardly, but as it straightened out they could see the van again, racing up the mountain.

"If we catch up to them, what'll we do?" Dave asked, swaying with the gathering speed of the bus. "Run them off the road?"

"If we run them off the road, we might hurt A. J. Plus, we can't take a chance like that with these kids on the bus," Steve called over the engine noise. "All we can do is try to get close enough to read their license plate. At most, we'll get a fix on what general direction they're taking him."

The engine labored as they struggled up the steep grade. The needle on the temperature gauge bounced to "HOT," then drifted back to the middle of the indicator.

Suddenly Steve let out an exclamation. "They took the other fork!" he cried. "Hold on!"

The bus twisted through a short series of curves, rocking side to side. An instant later, a fork in the road appeared. Just as Steve swerved right to take the fork, a yellow TR7 sporting ski racks zoomed by the right side of the bus, blaring its horn.

Steve jerked the wheel and slammed on the brakes. The rear end of the bus fishtailed to the right. The children screamed. Steve steered into the skid competently, and the bus hurtled into the turn-off.

"Stupid speed freaks!" Steve muttered. "That was close!"

"Steve!" Renee called from the back. "This is too dangerous! Let's go back and call the police!"

"By the time we get to a phone, they'll be long gone!" Steve shot back, pushing the gas harder.

Splendini!

High above them, maybe a mile ahead, they could see the van shooting toward a mountain peak. The last rays of the sun flashed gold from the rear windows.

"They're getting further ahead!" Dave cried. "We've got to catch up to them!"

"We don't have a chance on this uphill stuff," Steve bellowed. "They have almost twice the power we do. But once we get over the peak and head downhill, our extra weight might give us an advantage."

The van topped the peak and disappeared. Dave bit his lower lip in frustration. The other campers, who had originally demanded to know what was going on, now sat gripped by the high-speed chase. The din of the engine made most conversation impossible. Some of the children were crying.

"I have to slow down, Dave," Steve shouted over the motor. "We're starting to overheat! I could blow the engine!"

It seemed an eternity until they reached the mountaintop. For one brief second, they broke into a clear area, and Dave had a vivid panorama of the entire mountain range. Frozen in an instant of time, he saw the mountain shadows blanketing the valleys, in contrast to the peaks that glowed in the sun's last fiery moments. Like a ribbon, the highway curved and twisted along the slopes, doubling back on itself and cutting a thin line through the pines. Briefly, the golden sun seared his eyes; then they plunged into shadow on the east side of the mountain. The road sloped downward before them.

Steve shifted to a higher gear and the engine roar dropped, only to begin building again. "Now we'll get some speed," he promised.

It took Dave's eyes a second to adjust to the rapidly gathering night in the mountain shadow. Then, far below and to the right, he saw a tiny pair of headlights where the van sped on. "They're way ahead now!" he groaned.

Steve punched on the bus headlights. Startled, a squirrel

burst out of the underbrush and skittered across the road just in front of the bus. The bus bore down on it, and the small creature barely cleared the tires. Dave realized they couldn't stop now if they wanted to.

"We're gaining on them!" Steve cried. The headlights below seemed closer as they spiraled down the switchbacks.

Suddenly, a steep curve loomed into view. The headlights caught a sign that read "25" with a curving arrow. Again Steve jumped on the brake and twisted the wheel. The bus slid into the curve. As the rear wheels crossed over a patch of gravel in the road, they spun into another skid, and the rear end of the bus bounced off the rock outcropping next to the road with a nerve-shattering crash. For a moment, the bus slithered from side to side, out of control; then Steve reined it in and they plummeted on.

By now over half the campers were crying or near tears. "Stop the bus!" a boy pleaded.

"Steve!" Renee shouted. Her voice crackled with urgency.

Dave had an acid feeling in the pit of his stomach. The chase was getting out of hand. "Steve—" he began.

Just then the bus hurtled over a hump in the road and they found themselves staring almost straight down at the steepest grade they had faced yet. *"Hang on!"* Steve yelled and stomped the brake. But their momentum and the sheer grade would not let the bus stop.

The scream of the engine invaded Dave's fear, and he looked at the temperature gauge. The needle quivered, hovering far into the red. The laboring engine was slowing the bus more than the brakes. If it blew, they could plunge to their deaths!

"God, help me!" Steve prayed out loud. "Protect these kids!" The sweat drops on his face and forehead glistened in the light from the instrument panel. "I can't get the bus to stop!" Steve yelled.

Ahead, and down, the headlights picked out a narrow corridor of road. Another sign read "15" with an arrow pointing left. Behind the sign was a flimsy guardrail and behind the guardrail was a black drop into the valley from the outside of the curve.

Engine howling, the bus leaped for the curve as if attacking it. Steve stood on the brake and the clutch so hard that he lifted out of his seat. All four wheels froze, scraping across the road with an ear-splitting squeal as the bus fishtailed in a furious slide. Dave saw the guardrail flying straight toward them; then it rushed to one side as the bus spun in a half-circle. The snap of the wooden signpost came from behind them; metal scraped against metal. Suddenly, the back of the bus dropped a foot with a mind-shattering crash.

Reacting almost instinctively to the change of direction, Steve pressed the accelerator and popped the clutch. The bus jumped forward five feet, the motor died, and in the next second, something blew up under the hood. Scalding white steam poured into the cold night air, hissing and spitting.

The bus sat still.

For long moments no one moved. Only the steam broke the deafening black silence, scolding and babbling as the water boiled in the radiator. From the darkness that was the back of the bus came sobbing.

Dave found himself lying on his back, thrown down the three steps that led out of the bus, head pressed against the door, by the double impact, but he didn't seem to be injured. A ratchet sound told him that Steve had applied the emergency brake. Then Steve was offering him a hand. "Can you move, Dave?" his voice sounded quiet but impelling. "I have to open the door. We may be hanging over the cliff."

Dave took Steve's hand and allowed himself to be lifted to his feet. His neck muscles hurt all around, and his head ached where it had hit the door, but he felt all right. Dazed, he rubbed his neck and looked around.

Miracle and Disaster

He could hardly see. The mountain night seemed blacker than black with no street lamps or store lights around. He could just make out Renee, sitting in one of the seats with her arms around two girls who huddled into her from each side. "Is anyone hurt?" she called out.

Meanwhile, Steve hit the lever and folded the bus door open, bounced to the road outside, and ran for the back of the bus. Dave followed more slowly.

The bus was sprawled across both lanes of the road, headlights blazing into the pines. "Dave, look," came Steve's voice from the back of the bus.

Dave hobbled to the back of the bus. Steve pointed toward the ground several feet away where the warning sign that read "15" lay on its back in the dirt, broken. A few feet behind the bus, a splintered stump marked its former position.

"Look at the guardrail," Steve said. "It's bent out of shape. And look here—"

Dave stared in the red light of the bus's brake lights. Tread marks led straight from the edge of the cliff to the tires. The soft shoulder at the edge had a ragged chunk missing, and the yellow paint of the bus showed in broad lines along the white guardrail.

Dave's eyes widened. "We went over the edge!"

"Yes, one tire did," Steve said. "The shoulder held just long enough for me to drive forward a couple of feet, then fell away. And look what held us from sailing straight over the edge." Steve placed one foot against the battered guardrail and pushed with the slightest effort. A part of the rail snapped and dropped into the darkness. After what seemed an eternity, they heard a muffled crunch from far below. "That thing couldn't hold a fly, much less a bus," Steve said. He controlled his voice with difficulty. "It's a miracle!"

Dave caught on. "He answered your prayer! Your short little prayer! Just like you taught this morning—"

"Yes," Steve said ruefully. "I can't believe what I just did with thirty lives. But He answered my prayer. Come on, let's see if anyone's hurt."

They hurried back into the bus, and Steve turned on the overhead lights. "Is anyone injured?" he called.

"Banged up some, and scared to death," Renee answered, from where she knelt in the aisle beside one of the younger boys, "but no injuries. Everyone stayed strapped in." She couldn't resist adding, "The only casualty in this accident will be you when the parents hear what you did."

"It got out of hand," Steve said. "I'm sorry. I didn't want to lose A. J."

"A. J.!" Dave remembered. In vain, he searched the surrounding scenery for headlights. "Where is he?"

"A better question might be, where are we?" Barry interjected.

"Are we about to roll off the cliff?" Lisa asked. "I felt the bus drop!"

Other voices chimed in as the kids began to shake off the effects of the near-fatal ride. Steve lifted his hands for silence. "Wait! We can't roll over the cliff, and I don't know if the bus will run. But we're all right. No more questions until everyone stops crying!" He strode down the aisle to Timmy, who held onto Renee and shook with suppressed tears. "We're all right, Timmy. God kept us safe. And He'll get us out of here, too."

Timmy turned a tear-stained face toward Steve. "But why didn't God keep A. J. safe?" Timmy sobbed. "I'm scared!" He buried his face in Renee's arm.

"There, there," Renee said, "A. J.'s okay." Dave couldn't imagine where her confidence came from. "Even in 'the valley of the shadow of death,' Jesus is with us. And I want to thank Him for protecting us!" Right there, rocking Timmy gently, Renee led the group in a prayer of thanksgiving. When she finished, an air of calm filled the bus.

"All right now," Steve said. "I want to take a look at the bus engine. I'm sure I can get it working, and then we'll go for help. We'll probably only be a couple of hours late getting home. But I want everyone to stay on board so no one wanders off in the darkness. Renee? Want to sing?"

Renee ventured a small protest. "Chorus time! Again?" A couple of the girls managed a weak giggle. Before Steve could reply, Renee began singing, "The Lord is my Shepherd, I'll walk with Him always," and kids began to join in.

Dave followed Steve off the bus. "I can help, Steve," he offered.

Steve paused in his tugging at the hood. "All right. The flashlight is in the tool kit under the last seat in the bus. Would you get it for me?"

Dave nodded and jumped back into the bus. As he made his way down the aisle, he suddenly realized he was walking straight toward Sylvia.

"Excuse me," he mumbled awkwardly. "I have to get the tools from under your seat."

"Dave," Sylvia said without moving. Something in her voice made him look her straight in the eye as the singing continued in the background. "I don't like A. J. You know that. But—" She paused, as if what she had to say came hard. She pushed a loose red curl out of her eyes. "I never wanted anything like this to happen to him. I'm . . . sorry."

Dave stared in astonishment. He could see she really meant it. Suddenly the word "sorry" covered a lot of ground. "Thanks, Sylvia. Thanks a lot." He stooped and dragged the toolbox from under the seat. With an effort, he lifted it. "I'm sorry too," he said, hoping she would understand he wasn't talking about A. J.

She gave a timid smile. "I'll tell you one thing," she said. "For better or worse, you two certainly make it an exciting day camp."

In spite of himself, Dave had to laugh. For a moment he just looked at Sylvia, not knowing what to say or how to excuse himself. He didn't want to endanger the fragile possibility of friendship by saying the wrong thing.

Then Sylvia said, "Go fix the bus, stupid. Let's get out of here."

Outside, the mountain air nipped at Dave's damp shirt even through his jacket. Steve made a quick inspection of the engine by flashlight. He explained that the engine had died only because he had had it in the wrong gear when he let out the clutch after the skid. Apart from the overheating, they should be able to drive the bus. Dave suggested checking the thermostat, in case it had frozen shut and wouldn't let the water cool the engine, but Steve overruled him in favor of giving the water thirty minutes to cool. Then they would try to start the bus and see how it ran. All the tires and suspension seemed sound enough.

After they boarded the bus and Steve explained their situation to the rest, the group seemed to be more optimistic, and between songs there was even some laughter. But the atmosphere was still charged with the unvoiced questions: What had happened to A. J.? And why?

"We may be three or four hours late after all," Steve joked once, "because of how slooooooowly I'm gonna drive once we get going!" Everyone laughed, but Dave knew the joke was forced. He knew the parents would blame Steve for their situation, but he felt partly responsible. After all, A. J. was his friend. He had brought him to camp. And Steve had cared enough about A. J. to jeopardize everyone else to try and save him. And where does God's love fit into this? Dave wondered. If He could save the bus, why couldn't He save A. J.? His only answer was the mountain wind rattling the bus windows.

Steve had just decided to try the motor when a pair of

headlights came up the road from the opposite direction. Approaching the bus, the lights slowed to a stop.

"Oh, no," Steve said. "I've got the bus blocking the whole road." He scrambled into the driver's seat and cranked the ignition. The motor ground a few times and coughed hopefully, but refused to turn over.

"Give it more gas!" Dave called from where he sat with Barry.

A door slammed, then another, and footsteps crunched toward the bus. Headlights blinded them and kept them from seeing who approached.

"If I can't start the bus, maybe these people will help us," Steve said.

Heavy pounding shook the door. "All right, all right," he muttered, and began to open the door with the lever by his seat.

Without warning, the slowly opening door was bashed aside. Two men wearing ski masks and blue turtlenecks stormed into the bus. One of them held a high-powered rifle in his gloved hands and pointed it at Steve's head. "Don't anybody move, or this guy's dead," a deep voice threatened from behind the mask.

Everyone froze. Steve's eyes bulged at the barrel, inches from his face. Dave's heart pounded as though it would batter down the seat in front of him.

The second man pushed past the gunman. Shorter than the huge gunman, he wore a bulky down jacket over his turtleneck sweater. Without a word, he stalked the aisle, glaring one by one at each person.

Dave trembled, recognizing the smoldering eyes he had seen hours ago in the forest. Suddenly an earlier picture flooded his memory—one of an office turned upside down, and those same blazing eyes meeting his for a fraction of a second. With a rush of revelation, Dave realized what this must be all about, why they had kidnapped A. J. They had meant to kidnap *him! He* was the target. But the thief hadn't gotten a good look at him that day in the office. All he must have seen was *the blue hat!* And A. J. was wearing it now!

As the man came nearer, seat by seat, Dave stared straight ahead. He knew that under the mask must be a dark blond beard and a scar. He couldn't look at the man.

"Wh—what do you want?" Steve managed.

The rifle never wavered. "Not a sound," the gunman ordered.

The second man paused by Dave's seat. Dave held his breath, staring straight ahead. He felt the gaze drill a hole in the side of his head. Then the man moved on.

Within minutes, he had reached the end of the aisle and returned to the front. The gunman looked at him and the second man shook his head, "No."

"We want David Scott," the smaller man demanded. At the mention of his name, Dave's blood froze in his veins. "Which one is he?"

"He—he didn't come today," Steve stated, now bold enough to return the man's glare. "He's home sick."

The gunman's powerful arm delivered a vicious backhand to Steve's jaw. It snapped Steve's head to the side, and he let out a grunt. He turned to leap out of the seat when he found the weapon thrust into his face again. He froze.

"No games," the gunman commanded. He turned and addressed the group. "We want David Scott."

No one moved. No one answered. "NOW!" he shouted, and the rifle exploded blue flame. The back window of the bus shattered, bits of glass flying into the night. Sylvia screamed and dived to the floor.

"Sylvia!" Renee shouted. "Are you all right?"

Sylvia lay among the broken glass, choking back a sob. After a moment she managed, "Yes."

"Sylvia," the smaller man said thoughtfully. "Sylvia Johnson—or should I say, Carrington?"

A pause hung in the air. Sylvia sat up, brushed bits of glass off her arms. "So you know my real name," she said with defiance. "So what?"

"We didn't know you were in California," the smaller man said evenly. "You're coming with us, too." He hurried down the aisle and yanked Sylvia to her feet. Quickly he bound her hands behind her back, and covered her eyes and mouth with the black tape.

"Now," the man said, "for the last time . . . I want David Scott." And he pushed the rifle suggestively against Steve's temple.

Dave rose unsteadily to his feet. His throat felt as if he had gargled with sand, and his voice was just more than a whisper. "Don't hurt anybody," he begged. "Here I am."

In three broad strides, the second man reached Dave's side. He jerked him into the aisle and quickly tied his hands behind his back with short lengths of wire. Dave thought the wire would cut right through his wrists. Then, with a powerful shove, the man sent him reeling to the front of the bus.

"Don't try any heroics," the gunman instructed Steve. "We have others watching in the forest, and if anyone leaves this bus for the next two hours, this kid dies." While he spoke, the other man slapped black tape over Dave's eyes and mouth, just as they had done to A. J.

Plunged into darkness, face smarting, Dave felt another shove and stumbled down the steps to the ground. Strong arms hustled him across rough ground. A latch clicked. A hinge creaked. Suddenly he was lifted off his feet and tossed into a vehicle, landing heavily on someone else who grunted. He must be in the van with A. J.!

"A. J.?" Dave tried to say, but through the bandage it came out, "Mm Dmm?"

Splendini!

Another body fell on Dave, and a high-pitched grunt told him Sylvia had arrived. A door slammed.

Dave panicked as four gunshots sounded outside. Then he heard pressurized air whistling. They must have shot the tires of the bus.

Two more doors slammed. Someone started the van and spun it in a tight circle, causing Dave to tumble helplessly to one side; the other bodies crashed up against him. Then they roared off into the night.

Dave couldn't see, but all too vividly he could picture the yellow bus, lying crippled across the mountain road, headlights angled crazily into the pines. As the van raced away, the bus seemed to shrink and fade, until finally it was swallowed by darkness.

6

Dismaland

 Splendini gazed into an oval mirror, trying a spell to improve his complexion. He gave the magic gesture and then cried out in horror as he saw his nose and mouth melt.

Suddenly, in slow-motion, the mirror burst into flying bits as a particle bolt blasted it. Slowly Splendini threw up his cloak to protect himself; slowly the glass came flying at him. More lightning bolts flashed down around him, creating explosions near his feet, and ever so slowly Splendini ran for his life.

The narrow road stretched dark and straight before him. Behind, a van came hurtling at him, driven by a man with a beard and a scar. The van drew closer and closer until Splendini slowly turned to face headlights that rushed right into his face—

Dave landed with a sudden jounce that pulled him out of his nightmare. Thin, grimy carpet, smelling of grease, pressed against his cheek, and he realized he still lay in the back of the maroon van.

He tried to open his eyes. He couldn't. His neck muscles ached, and his head throbbed. His arms were numb, but the warm crush on either side reminded him that A. J. and Sylvia shared his dilemma. The dream still seemed real to him, and he shuddered.

What had awakened him?

The van bounced again, turning, slowing. For the first time in—how long?—the drone of the engine dropped slightly.

Where are we? he wondered. How long have we been traveling? It must've been hours before I fell asleep, and who knows how long I slept. Long enough to dream.

Over the engine drone came a voice from the front seat, a voice that Dave recognized as belonging to the smaller man of the two who had stormed the bus, the one he was sure was the guy he'd seen in his father's office.

"Unit One to Big Daddy. Come in, Big Daddy. Over."

A CB unit crackled and spit; then came an answering voice. "Big Daddy to Unit One. Ready for your report. Over."

"Progressing on our new schedule with the proper consignment of valuables. In addition to the dark item, our distributor added a special bonus of a red product. No extra charge, in light of the previous error. Over."

A pause from the other end as the information was absorbed. "Very good, Unit One. This does serve to rectify your mistaken pickup of the light-colored product. We are now more concerned about receiving the payment than delivering the goods."

"Message understood, Big Daddy. The red item guarantees we will have our payment before twenty-four hours, with an appropriate delivery to follow."

"Final delivery place and method is up to you, Unit One. Keep it under control if you value your . . . job. Big Daddy out."

"One out." Dave heard the CB go dead.

The van continued to slow, almost to a crawl. "Wonder why there's so much traffic at this time of night," a deep voice rumbled from driver's seat. "Roadblock?"

"Don't worry." This was the voice of the bearded man again. "Accident up ahead, that's all."

After a while the deeper voice said, "Poor sucker. No way he could have walked away from that . . . man, there's highway patrol everywhere."

"Relax. This van couldn't be hot yet. Not the way we left them stranded. The CHP is there for the wreck, not for us."

The van began to accelerate again. "Mighty sure of yourself, Keller. Too sure. That can be dangerous when you're playing with the big boys."

"I'm not playing with the big boys, Bronston," the one called Keller answered with deadly calm. "I am one of the big boys." After a pause, he added, "Biggest on the block."

"I know you like to think so," Bronston said. "But you heard Big Daddy's message. Another screwup like kidnapping the wrong kid and they'll kill you."

"Others have tried." Keller gave a short, nasty laugh. "Big Daddy's men are afraid of me. They know about the European kills. They remember that over there I was 'The Wolverine'."

"Over here you're just a street punk gone pro," Bronston said. "And I remember that, even with your French suits and—"

"That's enough." The voice cut like an icy knife, forcing compliance without using volume. The tone was filled with repressed violence, and Dave's fear grew.

Then the voice seemed to relax slightly. "I'm surprised you dwell so far in the past, Bronston. Just remember the grip this 'punk' has on you and keep your part of the act together."

"I'm in it for the money," Bronston snapped. "No one turns their back on a million-dollar cut."

"You can't lie to a liar, Dennis." Keller sounded almost

bored. "I know you planned to go straight. But you're too good at what you do—the best—and I wanted you. But don't tell me about money. We both know you're worried about what I'll do to the girl if you don't cooperate. And that's good. Keep her in mind, and you'll do just fine."

"Leave her out of this."

"You're soft, Dennis. It's a good thing you're getting out, because in this business you can't afford emotion. Emotion clouds your reasoning. The priority is survival."

"I'd rather be soft than psycho. Maybe someday you'll spend a month laid up in the hospital with nothing to do but think. I couldn't live with it. I'll never do this work again."

"After this job, you won't need to. You and your little angel of mercy can retreat to some far corner of the planet and live happily ever after." A trace of a sneer crept into Keller's voice. "Unless, of course, I need your services once ag—OW!" Keller drew his breath in sharply.

"I said leave her out of it," Bronston commanded as though through gritted teeth. "I'm doing your job. That means she's none of your business."

With quiet authority, Keller said, "Release my arm."

A pause. "Put that thing away," Bronston said. "I'm no good to you dead, and a wreck now would blow the whole operation."

"Release my arm."

Dave heard rustling sounds. Then Keller said in a low, menacing tone, "Don't ever touch me again. I am never without a weapon. I can easily replace you."

"Don't ever mention the girl again, Keller. I *am* a weapon. And I already want out."

Tension crackled between them for long moments. Then Keller began to chuckle. "Well," he said jovially, "maybe you're not so soft after all. I think we've reached a gentlemen's agreement. I won't mention the girl, and you won't employ your peculiar talents on me. *Laissez faire. Combien?*"

"Take your four languages and stuff it."

"But, monsieur! Le jour de gloire est arrive!"

"'Hour of glory,' my eye. Not until we get those hyperspace blueprints. And we can't expect any more help from that jerk at Compudat."

"He's spineless," Keller agreed. "But he has his uses. We need him a little longer, to make sure that they deliver authentic plans."

"What about the kids, once we get the plans?"

"You heard Big Daddy. It's up to me, and they want it kept under control."

"Meaning?"

"I told you, I can't afford emotion. I must remain untraceable."

"But, Keller, they're just *kids!* And they haven't seen our faces!"

"Don't act so righteous. You don't want that girl of yours to know how you've really made your living for ten years, do you? These three brats could destroy your new life even more effectively than I could. We have no choice."

Silence.

The van droned on, leaving Dave with nothing but the smell of grease and the riot of his thoughts.

They're gonna kill us! The words bounced around the walls of his mind, over and over, berserk with urgency. Pictures of all kinds of violent deaths flew through his brain, and Dave couldn't stop them.

Someone's got to save us, he thought. Steve saw us get kidnapped—but no, they left him stranded. We could be hundreds of miles away by now. . . . If my dad comes through with the plans, maybe they'll let us go.

He tried to cling to that, but the slender hope soon snapped like a thread holding a barbell. He felt certain the one called

Keller would kill them no matter what happened—plans or no plans.

Dave wanted to cry. The tears welled up, but the tape blindfold gave them nowhere to go. He fought to control his emotions, alternating between utter panic and a fierce kind of blind hope. Either way, the van droned along at the same speed. Finally he calmed enough to remember the Lord. He tried to pray, but he didn't know who to try and reach, or how the message had to be phrased. All he could think of were sing-song prayers from childhood:

> "God is great, God is good,
> Let us thank Him for this food;
> Thank Him for the birds that sing;
> *Thank* You, Lord, for *everything!*"

In the cruel darkness, the sugary prayers seemed almost stupid. I wish I knew God, Dave thought, really knew Him so I could talk and know He's listening. He's got to help us!

They're gonna kill us! The thought barged in and paralyzed his mind again.

He tried to swallow, and the pain in his throat pulled him out of the death-thoughts. His neck and head still ached from the tumble he'd taken in the bus. Somehow the pain restored some sanity. It was something real in his world of darkness.

So, Dave thought in a rational moment, there is an inside man at Compudat, and these guys think he's an idiot. I agree.

His thoughts turned toward his dad again. What's dad gonna do? He doesn't even know what's happened yet. Poor mom, when she finds out—

He visualized his mother and the comical way she talked to herself, narrating her own actions as she fixed dinner. The tears hammered to get out again.

And good old A. J., dragged into this mess because they thought he was me, Dave lamented. I was worried he might not go to church any more. Now he might not go anywhere any more! He might die! And what do they want with Sylvia? They seem to know her. Where are we going? How long have I been laying here? It seems like forever! Why did this happen, Lord? Why, why, why?

Time became a physical presence that sat on his back, shoving his cheek harder against the floor with each passing minute. He could hardly move, couldn't see, couldn't talk, couldn't feel his pinned-back arms. Sightless, motionless, he had nothing left to do but endure. Despite himself, he eventually dozed off again.

Unknown hours later, the back door rattled as a key thrust into the lock. A hinge creaked as the door opened, and a draft of fresh air washed into the van. It smelled of salt.

Rough hands grabbed Dave's ankles and dragged him across the floor of the van. Then he was outside, standing on his own feet. He could hardly balance.

He heard more dragging sounds. An indignant squeal told him Sylvia had received the same treatment. He heard tape being stripped off two other faces; then, without warning, rough nails scratched near his cheek and yanked the black tape off his mouth. The air felt cool on his face. Then they ripped the tape off his eyes, and Dave yelped; it felt like they had torn off a layer of skin.

He blinked and squinted. The world went from velvet black to searing yellow-white, with colors and shapes moving in and out. He closed his eyes, but explosions of orange and red still lit the inside of his lids. His eyes throbbed.

With painful slowness, his eyes adjusted, and he opened them a little at a time. Black prickles cleared from the edge of his vision, and he dropped his jaw in surprise at what he saw.

Remains, old and rotting, with a sour stench to prove it. It seemed more like a carcass than an amusement park.

Dead horses on the merry-go-round shed strips of cracking

paint. Abandoned skyway cars dangled from taut cables high overhead, helpless to stop the rust that relentlessly climbed steel stairways toward them. A paralyzed mockery of a Ferris wheel would never again spin lovers in lazy circles. Farther away towered a roller coaster where, years ago, drunken sailors had died; and the wind mourning in the thousand cross-supports seemed to make the park exhale a foul breath. Beneath it all, the ocean ate hungrily at the foundations.

Despite the warm sunlight, Dave shivered.

"Dave! It *is* you!" A. J.'s voice said from behind him. "What am I doing here? What's going on?"

A. J.'s eyes looked sunken in his lanky boy's face. Above the eyes and below the lopsided blue baseball cap, a lump showed where his forehead had struck the rock. His jeans showed stains from the dampness of his swimming trunks underneath, and his shirt was torn from his struggle with the kidnappers. His tragic T-shirted figure bore the label, "Pobody's Nerfect."

"It's a mistake," Dave said. "The hat. They thought you were me. I'm sorry."

"What is this place?" A. J. asked. "Where are we?"

Dave, A. J. and Sylvia huddled together and looked around. Straight ahead, two rows of buildings formed a midway, with various rides and attractions supporting broken signs. At the far end was a large open area and parts of more rides. One looked like a huge octopus head with crossed eyes. Giant tentacles jutted from the head, each with four cars on the end that could spin freely while the whole creature rotated and waved its arms up and down. A waist-high fence kept people out of the danger area of the rotating cars.

"This is Pacific Ocean Paradise," Sylvia stated. "Better known as 'P.O.P.'"

A. J. looked at Sylvia in surprise, then registered her presence with disgust. "This is worse than I thought. What are you doing here?"

"I might ask the same of you," Sylvia retorted. The kidnappers had taken her glasses when they covered her eyes, and she looked around with a permanent squint. One persistent curl drooped down her freckled forehead into her eyes, and she thrust out her lower lip and blew the curl to one side. It immediately fell back into her eyes.

The long building that formed the left side of the midway began near the trio with a "Hot-Dog-on-a-Stick" stand. A ladder leaned against the fading wall, and on the roof Bronston, the larger of the two kidnappers, suddenly appeared and began climbing down the ladder. The ladder sagged under his weight, but he looked like muscle, not fat. Dark hair fell past his collar in a loosely kept layer cut, framing a broad yet handsome face, and a tool belt jangled over his blue jeans as he jumped to the ground. He gave the teenagers one baleful glance, then resumed working with a length of wire and a phone receiver.

"Morning," A. J. tried. The man ignored them. "Please untie us," A. J. said slightly louder. "My arms are killing me."

"All in good time, *mon ami*," Keller said from behind them.

The three turned to look at the smaller man. The sea breeze pushed back his textured sport coat to show a silk shirt tucked into blue designer jeans. His sandy beard and high-fashion sunglasses hid much of his face, but Dave guessed the man must be in his thirties. Although Keller stood slightly shorter than A. J., his presence commanded attention.

"Welcome to our little fortress," Keller said amiably. "May I call your attention to the fact that there are only two ways off this island. One is behind you."

Dave turned and stared. Past a merry-go-round, past ticket booths, something like twenty acres of wide-open parking lot separated them from a gate, small in the distance. Through the gate he could see a road that turned into a mile-long bridge to the mainland; and across glittering water, sunbathers appeared as tiny clots of color on a strip of beach lined by more parking lots. His heart sank. No one over there would ever hear them, and they could never get across the parking lot and the bridge without the kidnappers noticing them.

"Aside from the bridge, the rest of the island stands approximately fifty feet straight up from the water, surrounded by shoals. The other way off is to plunge to the rocks below—a quicker exit, but an unfortunate accident for three curious youngsters who had no business exploring the island to begin with."

Keller impaled them one by one with steely grey eyes. "Which exit you take will be entirely up to you. Do I make my meaning clear?"

No one answered. Without warning, Keller delivered a sharp slap to A. J.'s jaw. "You, loudmouth—do I make my meaning clear?"

A. J. glared at Keller. A tiny trickle of blood dribbled from his lip. Sullenly, he said, "Like crystal."

Keller was all warmth again. "Good. You should also know that I am never without a firearm of some sort. Here at the park I have an office filled with weapons for both day and night use. I am an expert marksman. Observe." From inside his coat Keller drew a hand gun. It looked like a gun Dave had seen in a James Bond film, and he recognized it as a Luger. Keller glanced upward, selected a seagull gliding out over the ocean, almost in one motion raised both hands with the pistol and squeezed off a shot. The bird jerked and plunged toward the ocean, headless.

"You *beast,*" Sylvia gasped.

"Yes," Keller told her. "A wolverine, to be exact. You had best remember it."

A wave of fear shook Dave's body. The man had to be sick. At one moment, so refined, so polite—the next, heartless and proud of it. Dave knew then that they would never leave the island alive.

"You'll never get away with it," Sylvia snapped. "This island must have some sort of security patrol. When they find you here, you'll be turned in."

Keller gazed at Sylvia in mild amusement. "Thinking. Always thinking. That's good, although I'm not sure what it accomplishes in a child. The truth is, there once was quite a security force here when the park first closed. Over the last two years, it seemed less and less necessary, until they cut back to one caretaker. And that poor old gentleman had such a drinking problem—well, they were delighted to hire a man with as much electrical expertise as Dennis, here, to watch the place. He is the security guard." Keller threw back his head and let out a short, sharp laugh at the look of dismay that covered three faces.

"Dennis," Keller called, "is the wiretap ready? It's nearly time!"

"All set. I'll have Compudat on the line in just a moment." Dennis held a receiver in one hand, with wires leading to it from an old telephone line overhead. He punched a lengthy series of numbers, then held it to his ear, waiting.

After a moment, in respectful tones, Dennis said, "Yes. Dean Scott, please." He handed the receiver to Keller.

Dave's eyes widened. They were going to talk to his dad! If only he could think of a clue to pass on! But it would have to be something that his dad would understand and the kidnappers would not. He racked his brain, trying to find some code word, but the thought of the falling gull jammed his thinking process.

"Scott?" Keller said. "Listen closely, because I'll only say this once. I have your son, Carrington's daughter, and a friend of theirs in my custody, unharmed. If you want to see them again, alive, you must turn over to us the original copy of the

hyperspace projection blueprints that are now in your posses-
sion. All of them."

Keller paused for a second and listened. "Yes, I can prove it.
I'll let you talk to him."

The sandy-haired man turned and thrust the receiver against
Dave's ear and jaw. "Speak," he ordered.

Static crackled faintly in Dave's ear; then he heard a metallic
version of his father's voice. "Dave? Son, are you there?"

"Dad! Yeah, I'm here!"

"Are you all right, son?" Concern filled the tinny voice.

"Yes—" Dave gulped. His mind raced, trying to think of a
clue. "These guys are serious, dad—"

"Are A. J. and Sylvia unharmed?"

"We're okay." Dave concentrated furiously, but nothing
would come. His mind stuck on the image of a headless sea
gull.

"Listen, Dave," the voice urged, "trust the Lord. Have you
got that? *Pray and trust the Lord.*"

Dave saw Keller's grip tightening on the receiver. He was
about to take it away. Dave shouted, "Don't do what they say,
dad! They're gonna kill us—"

"Scott? You can see that he's all right. No, that last sen-
tence depends on you. Here are your final instructions. . . .
Don't try to stall, Scott; this call is untraceable.

"Put the plans in a briefcase and take them with you in your
car. Take Pacific Coast Highway north toward Agoura. Follow
the signs to the turnoff for the old Paramount Ranch. You'll
see a parking lot used for the Renaissance Pleasure Fair.
There's a phone booth in the lot. Be in it at eight o'clock
tonight and you'll get further instructions. Be sure to have
plenty of gasoline in your car. Don't tell anyone else about
this, and *come alone*—or you'll never see your son again."

Keller listened a moment more and his temper flared across
his face. He seemed to control himself with difficulty. "Scott, I

know you don't have authority to take the plans. Nobody has to know you took them. Your choice is clear. You can save your blueprints, or you can save your son. Don't make the wrong decision."

Keller nodded at Dennis, and the brawny man disconnected a wire and the receiver went dead.

Dave's heart sank. Due to his slow thinking, they had lost their only chance to plant a clue for outside help.

"Well?" Dennis asked. "Think he'll come through?"

Keller eyed the teenagers. "He'd better." He tossed the receiver to Dennis. "Time to lock up our merchandise. Bring the van around. You three, start walking down the midway until I tell you to stop."

With a last glance back toward the mainland, Dave turned and hobbled down the center of the park. The wind blew in his face, tossing the open front of his jacket against his arms. He had difficulty keeping his balance with his arms tied back; he longed to free them.

A. J. and Sylvia shuffled wordlessly on either side of him, and the light crunch of Keller's footsteps sounded menacingly behind them. His mind still worked double-time, frenzied with fear but trying to plot an escape. He scoured the surroundings with his eyes, groping for an idea.

To either side of the avenue were rides and cheap thrills. On the left, they passed some sort of fun house. Dave raised his head, trying to read the sign above the building. It said, "Laff in the Dark," with the *t* and *e* in "the" gone. On a platform near the roof, chipped mannequins of life-size clowns surrounded the sign. A fat lady in a red polka dot dress stood frozen with one arm holding her belly and another in the air, her head thrown back, her mouth wide open as if bellowing with glee. The arm in the air was missing the hand, and she looked as if she were wailing at her stump in the air.

Across from "Laff in h Dark," a boarded-up room advertised

skee-ball and pinball. Graffiti scrawled across paintings of prizes and dollar bills.

"Bring the whole family," A. J. murmured behind Dave.

"It's not exactly Disneyland," Dave agreed.

"I think 'Dismaland' might be more appropriate," Sylvia said.

To their left, they now found themselves passing "The Mirror Maze—Can You Find Your Way Out?" A padlock hung on the doorway, twisted and broken open.

At the end of the row of attractions, Dave could see the open area where the Octopus squatted, and beyond, artificial caves, rigged contests, a jungle ride, and the end of the skyway cars that hung overhead.

"Hold it!" Keller ordered. They had stopped near the remains of a food stand. Behind them, he stepped up five stairs that led to a locked door marked "Employees Only." After unlocking the door, he motioned them up the steps.

Dave stepped through the door into a darkened room. Sylvia and A. J. filed in after him and blinked in the gloom. Dave turned around just as Keller began to shut the door.

"Wait a minute," Dave begged. Keller paused. "What happens to us now?"

"You wait," Keller stated.

Mickey Mouse's voice said through Dave's mouth, "Then what?"

Keller shrugged. "You die." The square of light disappeared as he slammed the door and locked it.

7

Splendini Cannot
Save the World

Dave stood for a moment, fighting the urge to
cry. The only light in the room came from a
small window with a metal grill over it, near
the ceiling. He tried to turn and face the window, but his feet bumped something solid.

"A. J.," he said, "is there a light switch anywhere?"

A. J. stood closest to the door. Dave could just make him
out as a lanky shadow among lighter shadows.

"I'll check," A. J. said. "Just a minute." He seemed to
crouch and press his head against the wall as he stood up.

A switch clicked and a single, naked bulb in the ceiling
threw a glare down on them and their surroundings.

The room seemed the size of Dave's bedroom. One orange
wall, lined with shelves, held old cans of paint. Spare wheels
from roller coaster cars stood on edge in another corner. The
cement floor disappeared under stacks of large dusty cardboard
boxes labeled as napkins, paper towels, plastic eating utensils,
and toilet paper. The back wall, partially hidden by boxes,
held another door and gave out a steady, muffled hum.

Sylvia dropped tiredly onto one of the boxes. "Yech," she reacted. "Cockroaches." The sudden light and movement caused them to scurry under the boxes.

"What's the matter?" A. J. said sarcastically. "Afraid we might get germs and die?"

Sylvia stared at him in amazement. "Jokes," she said. "Nothing but jokes. Can't you tell this is serious?"

A disturbed look covered A. J.'s face. "I have to joke," he replied. "Otherwise I would just sit down and cry."

With difficulty, Dave made his way to a box and sat down. He felt like his body was full of lead. "What do we do, you guys?"

"Are you kidding?" Sylvia said. "First we have to find a way out of this room. Then we have to overpower two monstrous perverts, or sneak across a one-mile bridge and twenty acres of parking lot without them happening to notice us. Then we have to find someone who will help us, or find some police. All this with our hands tied behind our backs! 'What do we do?' indeed!"

"Would you rather just wait for them to kill us?" Dave fired back. "At least we have to try!"

"I don't know what to do," Sylvia said. "Leave me alone."

"Love to," A. J. said. "Dave, why don't we just step outside and give this lady her privacy?"

Sylvia struggled furiously to pull her hands out of the wire that bound them. "You little creep! Shut up!"

"You guys, you guys," Dave broke in, "this isn't getting us anywhere. I'm mad, too, but we can't fight each other. We have to work together."

Neither A. J. nor Sylvia replied. After a second, A. J. found a box and sat down, too. "Well," he said, "what do you want to do, Dave?"

Dave sat in silence for a moment. "All I can think of right now is getting my hands untied," he said. "I can hardly feel them. If we sit back to back, I think I can undo the wire on your wrists. Then you can untie me. You know, like in the movies."

A. J. stood up, turned his back to Dave, and scooted closer to him. "You want me to untie you first?"

"No, you've been tied the longest," Dave said. "Get closer. That's good. Now raise your arms a little."

Dave felt the wire. His own fingers seemed dead and unresponsive, and he had to close his eyes and try to picture what he felt. After five minutes of concentrated effort, though, Dave heard a small victory cry as A. J. pulled his wrists further apart. A second more and he was free.

A. J. folded his arms in front of his chest with a groan. "I can't feel anything," he said. "They're as dead as chunks of wood!"

"The blood circulation has to return," Sylvia said. "In a few seconds you'll feel more than you want."

They waited for nearly a minute. Then A. J. began to agree. "Here it comes. Ow, it feels like a million needles! Oh—" He gritted his teeth against the anguish and shook his arms violently trying to restore life as quickly as possible.

Dave watched helplessly. He couldn't massage A. J.'s limbs or offer any help until he was untied, and A. J. couldn't untie him until sensation returned to his hands.

After five or ten minutes, A. J. managed to rub his hands on his own arms, with limited success. Lines embedded in his swollen wrists clearly showed where the wires had been. "All right," he sighed. "Most of the pain's gone now. Your turn, Dave, but I'll warn you—the cure is worse than the disease."

Dave's bonds fell away much faster with A. J. able to see what he was doing. Soon the returning blood brought pain to his arms, too, but A. J. helped by chafing his wrists. By the time both the boys had freed themselves, they had already spent half an hour in the storeroom prison.

"Now," Dave said, "your turn, Sylvia." He turned to where she sat, faced away from them, aloof, with her back leaning against the wall that had the window. He didn't wait for her reply, but crossed over and began working at the wires. To break the tension between them, he prompted, "Tell us about P.O.P., Sylvia. How much do you know?"

Sylvia seemed to soften somewhat. "Obviously, it's an amusement park," she began. "Or was. We lived near here, years ago, and my parents brought me here often when I was little. I loved it then.

"But we stopped coming, for some reason, when I was only six or seven. I seem to remember my mom and dad talking about deaths on the roller coaster—cars that flew off a curve into the ocean. And there was a crime, or something—I can't recall. But the place finally closed until all the different lawsuits are cleared."

She shifted her weight so Dave could work faster. "Funny to be trapped here now, after all these years. We're finally back in California—"

Suddenly she cut herself off, as though she had been on the edge of revealing too much. The other Sylvia, the scientific one, reasserted itself.

"My favorite ride is called 'The Whirlpool.'" It has interesting inert and gravitational properties. A round room spins so rapidly that centrifugal force holds you to the wall when the floor drops." Her voice died away, as though she knew the sudden change of subject had been heavy-handed.

Dave exchanged looks with A. J. behind her back. Locked together with her in the tiny room, Dave felt he could only take so much of Sylvia's ultra-secrecy.

Dave had freed her hands while she talked, and now as life-giving blood announced its presence in her arms, her face reflected the flood of pain. Dave tried to massage her arms, but the girl shrank away from him. She folded her arms and rocked back and forth in misery until the pain subsided.

"Maybe we could swim for it," A. J. suggested hopefully.

"It looked like at least a mile to the mainland," Dave said. "I don't think we could make it."

"I can't swim," Sylvia added in a tiny voice.

"Figures," A. J. muttered.

"Let's move some of these boxes and see what's behind that other door," Dave said. "Maybe there's a way out."

Sylvia stood out of the way while Dave and A. J. shifted some of the boxes. Finally they exposed the door. It had a knob, but no lock.

Dave pulled it open and the throbbing of a huge engine filled the room. Before them sat a large motor, with belts spinning and gauges showing oil pressure, temperature, and the amount of gasoline in its tank. The tank was approaching empty.

"It must be their main power supply now that the place is closed," Dave said. "It's an electrical generator, gas-driven. It was probably a backup supply when the amusement park was open."

"Sure," Sylvia said. "If you were at the top of the Crow's Nest and all the power went out, you'd either fall to the ground or be stuck at the top unless there was a backup system."

A. J. whistled. "Can you imagine? One of the rides I saw sticks you to the wall—like Sylvia said, then raises in the air and spins sideways. If you were on that and it suddenly quit—" He left the rest unsaid.

"It's on low idle right now," Dave said. "Just enough to power a few light bulbs. We'd better close the door before the gas fumes fill this room." He shut the door against the sound. "Interesting. But that still doesn't get us off the island."

Dave sat down on a box again and fought depression. It

seemed as though the room closed in on him; he felt tense and restless.

A sound came from the window, a spatter of water on pavement. A. J. went to the window, climbed up on some boxes, and peeked out through the grill.

"Man," he breathed, "these guys are smart. "They're washing the maroon paint off the van."

"Let me see," Dave said. He climbed up next to A. J. The window was barely big enough for them to both look down on the van. "That pattern underneath the paint looks familiar."

As Dave and A. J. watched, the two men scrubbed away the water-based maroon paint. After a few minutes, Dave recognized the markings on the second coat of paint. "It's a telephone company van!" he exclaimed in a whisper. "It looks just like the ones the repairmen use!"

A. J. dropped down from the window and plopped onto a box close to the floor. "That does it," he said. "Even if Steve got to some help and described the van, no one can trace us now. We're lost." He leaned his elbows on his knees and sank his chin into his hands, defeated.

Dave kept staring out the window. Nothing could look more innocent than a telephone van. It would never be suspected, and couldn't really be distinguished from a hundred other vans. No one could follow the kidnappers now.

Dave sat down again. What's the use, he thought. We're just kids. We need help to beat these guys, and there's no help coming.

Dave had set cogwheels in his mind to work on an escape plan. Now they creaked to a halt. He felt stupid for even attempting to out-smart professional criminals, men who based their very survival on stealth and craftiness and brute force.

"I can't believe this," A. J. said. His voice sounded small. "I can't believe we're really going to die. We're not—are we?"

Dave picked up a piece of the wire that had bound him and used it to head off a cockroach that scurried between boxes. He shook his head in response to A. J.'s question, numbed by a problem too grave to comprehend. He was used to his parents dealing with all the major problems, and now that it was up to him, his mind retreated from such an awesome undertaking. All he wanted to do was sit still and hope blindly for rescue.

For a while he passed the time by blocking the cockroach's path, no matter which way it turned, and keeping it in a tight circle. After a while he thought, *There I am.* A little bug trapped by something too giant to understand. What's even more absurd is that if these guys win, they'll kill not only us, but possibly the whole world. What was it dad called it . . . "the ultimate weapon"? It's too much.

Even Splendini cannot save the world.

After a while Sylvia broke the silence. "Those wheels look rather heavy. Could we use them to batter the door down somehow?"

"Keller would hear us," Dave mumbled, knowing he didn't even need to say it.

He resumed tormenting the cockroach until he grew bored and let it get away. Eventually A. J. spoke up.

"Maybe we could use the generator," he tried. "Maybe we could blow it up, Dave, and the blast would make a way out."

Dave looked at A. J. just to see if he was serious. "Sorry," A. J. said. "It was just a thought."

Time dragged on, mostly in silence. Dave sat and twiddled his piece of wire. Sylvia pushed several boxes together and used them for a makeshift couch. A. J. paced back and forth and gave reports on the kidnappers' progress with the van. They had scrubbed every speck of maroon paint from the van and Keller had drilled holes in the van's roof. Later he used the holes to install some kind of braces on top.

Eventually, Keller and Bronston disappeared, but the van

stayed put. A. J. took the opportunity to climb up and yank on the metal grill over the window. Bolts held it securely to the wall.

Hours passed. Dave began to concentrate on the ache in his neck and the pit in his stomach. He hadn't eaten since lunch yesterday at Arrowhead, which meant he had missed dinner and breakfast already.

A. J. tapped idly on a cardboard box, got interested in the sound, and worked his way into a frenzied drum solo. Sylvia ordered him to knock it off, and that kicked off another argument between the two. They no longer fought about anything that mattered. They were frustrated, trapped, and they took it out on each other. Childish, acid discussions burned the afternoon away, droning on and on until Dave wanted to scream at them. He didn't. Yet.

As time passed, A. J. gave up arguing and displayed more and more nervous energy. He paced; he shoved his hands into his pockets and leaned against the wall; he complained about the lump on his forehead; he piled up a titanic stack of boxes just for the satisfaction of knocking them down; he opened some of the boxes to look at what was in them; he held up a fragile plastic fork and volunteered to fight their way to freedom.

Finally Sylvia burst out, "Would you please sit down and stop bouncing around the room? You're driving me crazy!"

A. J. turned from the paint can he had been examining and fixed his rare no-nonsense stare on Sylvia. Dave saw it and braced for another outburst.

"You know what?" A. J. said. "In the last couple of hours, I figured something out. Keller said that kidnapping me was a stupid mistake. The way I see it, they mistook me for Dave because I was wearing his hat. I was wearing his hat because you soaked me with water. In other words, I wouldn't even *be* in this lousy hole if it weren't for you!"

Sylvia worked her mouth for a second before sound came out

of it. *"Me? You're* the one who challenged me to a water fight! I can't help it if you lost!"

A. J. put the paint can back on the shelf and stepped closer to Sylvia. "Too bad it was just balloons," he said. "If I'd been throwing rocks at you, then you might've gotten what you deserved. Who do you think you are? You came out of nowhere and started threatening me. You act all high and mighty just because you know some words I don't!"

Sylvia began to protest. "I'm not finished yet!" A. J. nearly shouted. "I don't know who your father is, but I don't care if he's the president of the United States, it still doesn't mean you can treat me like dirt! You've insulted me, ignored me, lied to me, and caused more trouble than you're even worth! As far as I'm concerned, these apes can have you, because you're no friend of mine until you learn to apologize!"

"Apologize?" In a flash, Sylvia was on her feet and facing A. J. toe to toe. "Apologize? Let's set the record straight! The first day I met you, you hit me in the face with your stupid toy!"

"That was an accident—"

"Then you wouldn't leave me alone when I asked you to! Then you and Klutzini over here held a gossip session about me with the head of your useless church!"

"It's not my church," A. J. said. "And we didn't—"

"Then, you tried to hurt me in a contest where you knew you had an unfair advantage! Lucky for me, Renee guessed what kind of coward you are and helped me out or you would've embarrassed me in front of everyone again! And as far as threatening you, I tried to *warn* you about the very situation you're in now! Just like I said—you're in horrible trouble, unexpectedly, and there's no one but yourself to blame! So why don't *you* apologize to *me* and then go join your fellow cockroaches under one of those moldy boxes!"

Anger paralyzed A. J.'s speech. Sylvia's attack was so unfair that he didn't know what to tackle first.

Splendini!

"You know what's the worst thing about this," A. J. said after a moment. "You keep saying your dad is so important. And I know Dave's dad is important. My dad's a paramedic, but off-duty he's mostly a drunk. I don't even know what we're here for. You two top-secret snobs won't even tell me what these idiots want. How come *I* have to be the butt of this?"

Dave avoided A. J.'s glare. He already felt a twinge of guilt because he had not told the other two about the conversation he had overheard in the van. Who should he be loyal to—his father or A. J.? He tried a dodge. "Tell him what they want, Sylvia."

Sylvia merely snorted.

Just then the lock rattled and the door swung open. Bronston stood in silence, studying them. He clutched a brown paper bag in one hand and had a pistol jammed into the waistband of his jeans. A. J. and Sylvia, not sure what to do, sat down on the boxes. Dave resisted an impulse to shove his hands behind his back and pretend he was still tied up. The wire was all over the floor.

The big man remained in the doorway for long moments, simply staring at them one by one. Finally a flip of the wrist sailed the brown bag into A. J.'s lap. "Burritos," Bronston stated. "You're probably hungry. And here's your glasses; I found them in the van." He tossed them at Sylvia, who surprised herself by accidentally catching them.

The three sat motionless, not sure what reaction would be safe.

Bronston stared back, his expression unreadable. Daylight streamed into the room from behind his broad back, like a symbol to Dave that they would have to get past him to get to freedom. The man's well-defined bulk pushed Dave's hopes even lower.

Finally Sylvia broke the silence. "Why do you keep staring at us like that?"

Dennis seemed unable to focus. "Because I'm not sure what

to do about you," he murmured vaguely. "My victims have always been a bank or an insurance company or men trying to kill me, but never. . . ." He trailed off, lost in thought, then suddenly snapped to. "I'm not about to start talking to kids about it," he barked. "Eat your food. We might need you to talk to Scott again later, and we want you in good enough health to do it."

"We'll eat for ourselves, not for you," Sylvia retorted as he turned to leave. "We'll use our good health to see you arrested."

Dave winced at Sylvia's pointless defiance.

The man turned stony eyes upon her. "You keep talking like that, sweetheart," he said. "It makes my job a lot easier on me." The door slammed shut with a heavy thud.

Dave and A. J. exhaled pent-up tension. "Sylvia! What did you do that for?" A. J. said.

"Because I hate them!" Sylvia stormed. "Just because they've got guns and muscles, they think they can do anything they want! It's not fair! We never did anything to them! This is all so—so—wrong, something's got to happen. Someone's got to save us."

"Look," Dave said, "I didn't say anything about this sooner because I didn't want to scare you more. Last night in the van, I was awake part of the time and I heard them talking. Keller plans to kill us no matter what, whether my dad gets the plans or not. But Bronston isn't sure he wants to do it. Let's not get him mad!"

"We think alike," A. J. said to Dave. "I was awake some last night, too. And I don't want Dennis mad, either. He's into martial arts."

"So," Sylvia defended herself.

"So," A. J. said, "he knows over a hundred ways to kill us with his bare hands. And you're helping Keller talk him into doing it."

8

Sylvia Tells All

Slowly the realization of what she had done filled Sylvia. She struggled to keep her fear from showing. Although she turned her back to them, Dave thought he heard a soft plop that could be tears hitting dusty cardboard.

Ignoring Sylvia, A. J. tore into the bag of burritos. Then the hungry teenagers temporarily forgot their situation and attacked the food like a pack of ravenous wolves. In two minutes the food was gone, except for finger-licking.

"There's so much to think about," Dave said around the final smack of his lips. "Something that's been puzzling me is why Bronston and Keller kidnapped you, A. J. We assume it was probably mistaken identity. But somebody followed me and my dad home from the magic shop Monday night. If it was Bronston and Keller, they'd know what I look like. If not them—who?"

"Is that what was bothering you yesterday?" A. J. asked. "When you sat on the bench at Arrowhead? Somebody had trailed you home the night before? Why didn't you tell me?"

Dave sighed. "I'm sorry. I couldn't tell you about it. You aren't supposed to know that Compudat has a top-secret defense project, much less that thieves would kill to acquire it."

"You've got some nerve," Sylvia announced. She sat bolt upright on her cardboard couch, obviously recovered from her shock. "You sit there and blab everything you know about our national defense, while your friend does everything to me but accuse me of killing us. I'd do anything to get out of here now, just to get away from you two."

Dave's eyes blazed, but he held himself in check. He knew that he'd feel sorry later if he slapped Sylvia now. But something told him it was time to find out Sylvia's secrets.

"Look," Dave countered, "A. J. made a good point before Dennis came in. Here he is locked up with us, and he doesn't even know what's going on. If he's going to die for it, he deserves to know." He turned to A. J. "I don't know that much about it either, A. J. But what they're after is a new weapon. It has something to do with particle beams."

Suddenly Dave had more of A. J.'s attention than any teacher had ever commanded. "Particle beams? What are those?"

Sylvia interrupted, nearly shouting. *"It's not your secret to tell!* It's government work, and it's classified! You can't decide who gets to find out!" She rose to her feet and stood with her hands on her hips, a stern look compressing her lips.

A. J. rose to his feet, too. "Then how is it you know so much about it?"

"That's different." Sylvia stumbled over her answer. "I learned it by accident. My father—" Again she seemed to feel she had revealed too much, and she shut up.

"Yeah, your father," A. J. sighed. He turned and sat down. "Go ahead and tell me the rest, Dave."

"Your father," Dave said, ignoring A. J. "I know what he does."

Splendini!

Sylvia looked startled. "You *do?*"

"Sort of. I mean, it's fairly obvious by now. Not every kid studies the gravitational properties of amusement park rides, and goes to a place like Compudat and asks 'questions with the wisdom of an insider.' Your dad's a scientist, and I wouldn't be surprised if he works for Compudat, too. Am I right or am I right?"

Sylvia looked agitated. "Please don't," she said. "I can't tell."

"Dave said before that we'd all have to work together," A. J. insisted. "I think it's time we all know what's going on and stop this 'I've got a secret' nonsense."

"Maybe we'll get an angle if we all know why we're here. And here's something else," Dave added. "It's obvious that the people who can cause trouble if they know who your dad is, and if they know about Compudat's business, already know. Your secrets are out, and they're already doing something about it. It's silly to hide it now."

Sylvia's expression stayed the same, but she sat back down on her box and mumbled something in a tiny voice. It sounded like, "You might be spies."

Dave startled all of them, even himself, with a sharp command. *Come on, Sylvia!* Darn you, half your secret is out already! Tell it to us!"

Suddenly he noticed that tears fought to escape Sylvia's tightly shut eyes. She took her glasses off and put a hand over her face. A sob broke from her throat.

My gosh, he thought, *what did I do?* Maybe I should back off—

"I'd love to tell you!" Sylvia said, and she began to weep in earnest. Through her tears she choked, "Oh, I'd love to tell you! You can't imagine how hard it's been, not talking to anyone for months and months about my family that I'm so proud of—" Her emotion overwhelmed her for a moment.

Finally she gave a long, robust sniff, wiped her face on one arm, and replaced her glasses. "You're right, of course," she said. "It can't matter now. And you're right, my father is a scientist."

A. J. couldn't resist exclaiming, "Hey! Now we're getting somewhere!"

Dave motioned for him to be quiet, but Sylvia said, "It's all right, Dave. A. J. acts like most people everywhere I've lived. I know I'm different."

"Not really," A. J. said. "If you look behind the 'reprehensibles' and 'centrifugals' and 'inerts', you're just the common, everyday, teenage genius."

Sylvia giggled through her tears. "I'm afraid I do talk differently, but I'm not putting on airs. I can't help it! It's what I hear at home. You see, my father is the foremost authority in the world on laser and particle beams."

A. J. looked goggle-eyed, but Dave took the news in stride. He made a statement in the form of a question. "He's in the Gang of 53, isn't he."

Sylvia looked a bit surprised at the reference, but nodded. "That's right. He generally works for the government, and they transfer him to wherever they need him for each project. For most of my life, we've moved two or three times a year. That's why I never have many friends, and I don't do too well at meeting people, anyway." Her eyes clouded with tears again. A. J.'s face softened. "So I retreat to my books, and scientific studies, and I write poetry and play guitar. Things I can do alone." She gave a feeble cough and added, "'Alone' seems made for me." She paused and wiped her nose with the bottom of her blouse for lack of anything else to use.

Dave said, "But what's scandalous about that? Why can't you just say, 'My father is a scientist'?"

Sylvia shook her head "no," swallowed a lump in her throat, and said, "The government projects are always top-secret. In his field, my father is well-known. The government is afraid that if foreign spies know where my father is, they'll guess the nature of the projects. Especially the hyper-space transmitter; it has more destructive potential than any weapon humanity has devised. A huge group of scientists is gathering around Compudat now, and if other countries knew who these scientists were, the secret would be deduced."

"It looks like it has been," Dave said. "That's the strange part. My dad told me hardly anyone in this nation knows about the project."

"I think there's an inside man," Sylvia said. "A traitor at Compudat."

"Me, too," Dave said.

"But there's more to my story," Sylvia went on. "I want A. J. to hear this part. My dad moved to Costa del Mar months ahead of my mom and me. When he left us, he couldn't even tell us where he was going, but he'd already clued me in on the nature of the project because I figured most of it out anyway from notes he left lying in his study. After a while there was some kind of dispute between my mom and the government. She's—well, a very strong lady—and she was tired of not knowing about my dad half the time, especially when it isn't even wartime. She wouldn't tell me what happened, but she made a lot of noise, and the compromise was that we got word from a government representative to move to this area. I'm sure my father is involved with Compudat somehow, but the thing is—we haven't heard a word from him since he moved out here. I haven't seen him for four months, and now that I've met these kidnappers—I don't even know for sure that he's alive."

A. J. whistled. "Then that's why you cried so much about a tap from a Frisbee," he said. "You had just moved here and still no word from your father, so the worry—"

"That's right, A. J.," Sylvia said. She looked at him with

red-eyed sorrow. "The pressure made me blow up. Then I got mad at myself, because by crying so much, I drew everyone's attention—"

"And no one was supposed to even notice you were in town," Dave finished for her. "That's why you said, 'I can't fail my father.'"

Sylvia nodded. "The worst part was that my mother had to get a job because there was no word or income from father. And all the secrecy made her worry about leaving me alone, so she had me go to the church day camp. Thirteen years old and I had to have a crowd of baby-sitters," she added bitterly.

"That sure explains a lot," Dave said.

"But then why did you threaten us on the bus?" A. J. asked.

"Oh, A. J., it wasn't meant as a threat. You two kept making such a fuss about me. And I didn't want to be noticed. It was just a clumsy attempt to make you leave me alone."

"Sylvia, I'm really sorry," A. J. said sincerely. "If I'd known any of this, I wouldn't have given you such a hard time."

"It's all right," Sylvia said. "It all sounds so improbable. I don't blame you for thinking other things. And by acting so weird, I didn't make it any easier for you." She wiped her eyes, then looked straight at him. "A. J., I know we're different, but our problem has mostly been misunderstanding. Can we be—I mean, if it's not too much trouble, could we—couldn't we be friends?"

"Friends?" A. J. said. Then he smiled. "Sure!" he said. "Of course we can!" Suddenly A. J. looked very serious and said in a low voice, "But we have to keep it a secret. Some people are the jealous type. You know what I mean?" A. J. jerked his head in the direction of Dave.

All three of them let out a relieved laugh. It was short and light, but it seemed to cleanse the room. "You two had better include me," Dave said. He changed his voice in an imitation of Sylvia's. "Or you'll be in horrible trouble—unexpectedly. Mainly, I'll slug you both in the nose."

They all grinned at each other. Then Sylvia sobered and said, "But if we ever get out of here—you must promise to keep my secret! You can't tell anybody who my father is!"

Dave and A. J. promised solemnly. "But," A. J. added, "that's not the whole secret yet. I still don't know what a particle beam is and why I might get killed because of it."

Sylvia grimaced, seeming to fight within herself over revealing even more forbidden knowledge. She stared down at her hands in her lap and found them twisting the tail of her sleeveless blouse into a knot.

"Please," Dave said.

"Particle beams," Sylvia said. She sighed. Then she looked at A. J. and said, "Small pieces of atoms—protons, electrons, and neutrons—concentrated, focused, and shot at high speed like an energy bolt. While scientists dealt with how to manipulate such small particles, they made a bigger discovery."

"Give me the dummy-English version," A. J. hedged.

Sylvia flashed a tight smile. "All right. The idea is that you take an object or a quantity of energy and manipulate the tiny particles that make it up. You put the particles in perfect electromagnetic harmony with some other point in the universe. It works like creating a miniature black hole around the object; it disappears here, travels through hyperspace, and instantly reappears at the distant point, drawn by the electromagnetism."

Her audience sat without speaking, straining at mental indigestion.

Finally A. J. said, "Hyperspace?"

"Yes," Sylvia said. "Hyperspace." She stared back at his blank expression, looking as though everyone knew the term. "You know—hyperspace!"

A. J. shook his head numbly. Sylvia ran one hand back through her hair, pushing her curl out of her eyes. "It's another dimension," she tried. "Space and time are completely different there, but it's still real. Like—like your thoughts. Your thoughts exist in another dimension."

"Wait," Dave said. "Thoughts are chemical and electronic impulses within your brain cells."

"That's the *way* you think," Sylvia said. "But the thoughts themselves don't exist here at all. If you're thinking about something that's true but not physical—a concept like justice, or love, or freedom—you don't look for two quarts of justice or a foot and a half of love, because they exist on a different plane. Hyperspace is like that—different, but just as real."

"I guess I don't care how it works," A. J. concluded. "The important thing is that it does work or we wouldn't be *here*. What's so terrible about the concept, then? What does it do?"

"Suppose someone in the Kremlin has one of these hyperspace transmitters," Sylvia said. "They're also called 'tuning devices' or 'resonance fields'. Suppose they blow up a nuclear warhead, but in the split-second before it goes off, they pop it into hyperspace. They already had their instruments all tuned, and the explosion instantly reappears in the White House. There's no plane, no tank, no missile—no warning at all. How could you stop it?"

Dave and A. J. sat slack-jawed for a moment. Then, "You couldn't even be sure who sent the thing," Dave murmured. "You wouldn't know who to fight!"

"Right. And it works another way, too," Sylvia said. "Theoretically, you could focus the hyperspace transmitter on an object and bring it to you. You could steal all kinds of weapons and secrets if you could just tune in to their electromagnetic pattern. Possibly make people vanish, too, only I'm sure it would kill them. Even at that, it would be the perfect method of assassination. Press a button, and pfft—no more president!"

"I can't believe all this," A. J. exclaimed. "Something like this must be worth billions of dollars to other countries! No wonder our lives are nothing to these guys."

"My dad said it was just talk and blueprints," Dave said. "Is any of this really happening yet?"

"No one is sure," Sylvia said. "Rumors. A huge explosion that blew up several acres of forest in Siberia, with no explanation. A submarine that suddenly bent itself sideways, in half, killing the entire crew when the shell cracked and the water flooded in. Who's to say what really caused it?"

Dave shook his head, as if rousting himself from a nightmare. "We've got to get out of here," he said.

Another realization hit him like a kick in the gut. "My dad's pretty smart. He knows our three lives aren't worth the lives that this knowledge could destroy. Even though he's my dad, he'll never hand over the plans. I wouldn't want him to." He paused. "So we know they'll have to kill us."

Nodding assent, Sylvia added, "The most logical thing to do would be to kill us one at a time. Then they leave the body to be found in some public place as a warning that another death follows if the government doesn't give in. It would put tremendous pressure on your father, almost as though he were responsible for each of our deaths."

"Man," A. J. exhaled. "How can you think such things?"

"I don't like to," she said. "It just makes sense, that's all. Keller doesn't seem like the squeamish type."

"We've got to get out of here," Dave repeated.

He hoped that no one would ask, "How?"

★ 9 ★

Splendini Tells All

Splendini cannot save the world.

The thought had occurred to Dave hours ago, but now it stuck in his mind like a one-line song.

He sat on a box again, wire in hand; only this time he tormented a silverfish instead of a cockroach, and his thoughts darkened his mood even more than before.

So this is being a Christian, Dave thought ironically, after nearly an hour of dejected silence. Pimples and clumsiness are bad enough problems, but look what happened after I got God in my life. His own helplessness sat on him like a ton of railroad spikes.

Splendini cannot save the world.

Why do I feel like it all rides on me? Dave wondered. Somehow I feel it's my fault that we're here. Keller saw me in dad's office. If I hadn't played hero, Keller would've gotten the papers and this would all be someone else's problem. Someone professional, like a CIA man. Someone adult.

I'm afraid my dad might give them the blueprints anyway,

just to save me. Then if the world blows up it's because of me. And if he doesn't. . . .

Dave didn't let himself think about what would happen then.

Here I was worried about whether or not I could handle a car payment in two or three years, after I get my license. That seemed like a nice mature problem. Or what to do in college, what kind of career to pick. Now the question is how to live through the next two days. God, I'm scared.

Splendini cannot save the world.

Dave nearly groaned out loud at his depression. He felt so confused. He had thought that becoming a Christian would mean the end of all his problems, but it had been just the beginning of them. All through this he had wanted to know God better, to find out how to relate to Him. As Big Buddy? Or as Sir? Or as The Force? And it seemed like God had only frustrated his efforts.

He thought of his father's last words to him, metallic and distant. "Listen, Dave. Trust the Lord. Have you got that? *Pray and trust the Lord.*" Click.

How do you do that, Dave wondered.

And then it hit him.

He had wondered if he had to wait until it was life-or-death before he bothered God in prayer. But this *was* life-or-death.

Splendini cannot save the world.

But he knows someone who can.

It seemed remarkably like a breath of fresh air; so much so that he was afraid to let himself believe it. But there was no other way to go. He took a deep breath.

"You guys want an escape plan?"

A. J. had been standing on two boxes, chin on the window sill, gazing out at the sunset. He kept staring straight ahead. "No," he said hopelessly. "Just someone to help me make out my will. I have a lot of valuable baseball cards."

Sylvia didn't answer, but gazed quizzically at Dave.

He paused and swallowed. "I know what we can do."

A. J. looked at him. "Really?"

Dave nodded.

A. J. jumped down off the boxes and walked over to him. "Well! The magic man comes through! Let's hear it, buddy!"

"Here it is," Dave said. "We're going to pray."

A. J. and Sylvia waited a full thirty seconds before they realized that was all he had to say.

"PRAY!" Sylvia cried. "That's it? What good do you think that'll do? You think we'll get a lightning bolt to blast the lock off the door?"

"After what you've told us, that's entirely possible," Dave said with a firm gaze at Sylvia. She looked nervous.

A. J. looked mystified. "Dave, you gotta be kidding! I mean—" He trailed off, at a total loss for words.

"I've never been more serious. I didn't tell you before, but—" He couldn't think of an easy way to say it, so he just blurted it out. "I'm a Christian now."

A. J. slapped his forehead and leaned back against his boxes. "No, Dave, don't tell me they got you. You know that stuff doesn't work!"

"No, I don't know that, Dave retorted. "I thought I knew that, but I never tested it before."

"A. J.," he said. He stopped and tried to find words. "A. J., I've been scared to death that you'd find out I changed my mind about Jesus. My body's changing and I feel weird and clumsy and I need every friend I can get. But darn it, I've been listening to you two fight for at least five hours, and I suddenly realized, look at these people! You're afraid of their opinion, and look what they've got! Nothing! And I can't tell you all about God because I don't really know anything about God, except what Steve's told me. But He's supposed to love us and

I know it's true, and I don't care what you think. We've got nothing else to try."

"But, Dave—" A. J. began.

"I know," Dave said. "Sometimes I feel almost like a traitor to the team. We've always thought pretty much alike."

"Yeah. That's what I want to say. I mean, it's always been us over here and religious people way over there. But now you—!"

"But it's not like teams or armies, A. J. It's more like—oh, I don't know, like we're all a bunch of homeless bums and some of us found some free food. I'm not better than you because I ate. Just happier. And I'll live longer. You know?"

A. J. shrugged. He looked very sober. "It's all right, Dave. I just hope—well—it makes me feel like you might get weird or something." He changed the subject. "What about your plan?"

"I want to pray," Dave said. "I'm new at this, but if we ask God to get us out of here, He just might do it. You want to pray with me?"

"I'm not ready to do that yet," A. J. responded. "I like action, not religion and rules and prayer."

"But it's not like you think, A. J., really it's not!" Dave felt a growing excitement. "I don't have to use 'thees' and 'thous' and 'thuses'. He understands *me*. The things that matter to *me!*"

"Like I said, Dave, if it works for you, great. I'm just not sure that I'd get anything out of it."

Dave leaned forward on his box. "Look, A. J., all I want to do is pray. I mean, you sure don't have anything to lose— well, there is one thing, but that's what we're trying to get away from. And if He gets us off this island safely, doesn't that prove He can help us every day? Wouldn't that prove He'll do the things we can't?"

"Sure," A. J. said. "*If* He gets us out of here. That's like bringing us back from the dead, just about. But that's a big 'if'."

"What about you, Sylvia?" Dave said, turning to the red-head.

"I'm sorry, Dave," she said. "Even if you come up with your miracle, I still don't believe the Bible. And—I wouldn't feel quite right turning to God now that I'm in trouble, when I never did before."

"I don't think He cares about that," Dave replied. "I'm gonna pray anyway. I don't expect either of you to join me."

Dave bowed his head. Suddenly he felt awkward and hesitant. When he spoke of God out loud, it sounded glorious, spiritual; but inside, he felt this was more of a desperate bid than anything else. Still, Dave thought, turning to God is turning to God, whatever the reason. But what do I say now?

"God," he said. It sounded cold and harsh in the suddenly quiet room. Dave changed it. "Dear Father," he said, "this is Dave." Sylvia sighed, and Dave realized, *That was dumb. He knows who I am. Forget the words. All that matters is what I mean.*

"We need your help, Lord." He tried to reach out and feel God there, but there was nothing; except—maybe a distant glimmer of faith. "These men say they're going to kill us. We know they want to sell a deadly invention. Jesus, get us out of here. Keep the plans safe, and keep us safe, too—like you did when everyone was in the bus and we almost crashed. And help A. J. and Sylvia to know you the way I do—the way I'm starting to." Dave thought for a second, and drew a blank. "That's all." He opened his eyes, then suddenly remembered the proper ending, and quickly closed his eyes again. "In Jesus' name. Amen."

As Dave looked up, he felt a burst of exhilaration. He felt relief. Now things rested in more capable hands than his. Sylvia wiped the feeling away with two sour words.

"Now what?"

Dave just looked at her. He looked at A. J. He looked over

at the door. Then, feeling stupid, he went over to it and rattled it. The lock held tightly as ever.

Dave gave an apologetic shrug. "I don't know. It's uh, not really up to me now."

Sylvia gave a rather nasty laugh and turned her face away. Dave blushed. He felt exactly the same as when he had dropped his best magic trick while performing for the entire sixth-grade class. He sidled along the wall and sat on a box in the furthest corner.

They waited.

After a while A. J. ventured, "Maybe you should have given him a time limit."

"I'm not sure I can do that," Dave said. "It's not like I can make demands. But I have another idea. Maybe He wants to use us, instead of doing it all Himself. Maybe it is up to us, but now He'll help us."

"We thought of everything we could," Sylvia grumped. In an over-dramatic voice she added, "We're doomed."

"No," Dave said. "We've just got to think harder. We just need some more ideas."

"All right, we'll think harder," Sylvia said resignedly. "We've got our hands untied. Now we have to break that lock and get rid of Laurel and Hardy out there."

A. J. frowned in concentration. "We don't have to worry about opening the door if they do it for us," he realized. "Maybe I could hit one over the head with a can of paint."

"Hmm," Sylvia said. "But we'd never be able to get them both that way, and then they'd be mad. They'd kill us."

"The only other method is to try to sneak away," A. J. said. "We'd have to wait until dark, and we'd have to have a quiet way of getting out."

"The window's pretty small," Sylvia said, "but we might be able to squeeze through it if we could get those bolts off."

"Yeah, but we'd need a wrench," A. J. said. "Wait a minute!" He stood up and went to the door to the generator. The throbbing filled the room again as he opened the door and went inside. After a moment he returned, discouraged. "I thought maybe they'd have a wrench in there for working on the engine. No good."

After a minute's silence, Sylvia said, "Maybe we could hide when they return and convince them we've already escaped. Then when they go to look for us, we'll slip out."

"That's a dumb idea," A. J. said. "Where would we hide in a tiny room like this?"

"Well, it's better than your ideas!" Sylvia accused. In a nasal tone, she imitated A. J. "'Dave, let's blow up the generator!' A. J.—" She stopped herself. "I'm sorry."

"I understand," A. J. said softly. "Being cooped up in here makes me get crazy, too."

Suddenly the sound of the van's engine burst into the room. They all looked at the window, startled. A. J. bounced to his feet and scrambled across the room. In an instant he had his face pressed to the metal grill. "It's Bronston," he reported. "He's leaving! He's got some ladders on top of the van and he's pulling away."

"Of course!" Dave exclaimed. He snapped his fingers. "Sure! He's going to collect the hyperspace plans from my dad! He'll probably tap into a phone line somewhere and call that phone booth!"

"But," Sylvia said, "I know basically where P.O.P. is, and I know where Agoura is—I went to the Renaissance Fair. He'll be gone for at least an hour."

A slow smile spread across Dave's face. "Good! That's part of the answer to the prayer, then! One guard out of the picture!"

"Hey!" A. J. said. "Yeah!"

"Not so fast," Sylvia said. "He would have had to leave anyway, even if you didn't pray."

"I guess," Dave admitted. "But we didn't know that when I prayed, and things are getting better." He leaped to his feet and began pacing the room. He felt excited for some reason. "There's only one guard now," he said. "And he can open the door for us."

A. J. scrambled down the box ladder. "Back to the 'hit-em-on-the-head-with-the-paint-can' bit."

"No, Keller's much too experienced to fall for that. But I know he doesn't expect much out of us 'mere children.' Maybe we can take him totally by surprise."

"I wish there were some way to bribe him," Sylvia said. "They use that in movies."

"Maybe he'll let us go if I show him how to make a rabbit vanish," Dave muttered. He paced past the door of the generator and felt its hum. There was plenty of power under restraint in there. "Magic," he murmured. "Some good old magic. Let's see—"

Preoccupied, he shoved his hands into his jacket pockets. Something hard and square greeted his right hand.

"What's this—"

It dawned on him.

"I've got it!" he exclaimed. "I've got the plan!"

"Let me guess," Sylvia said. "Now you want to take up a collection." Her smile this time showed genuine good humor.

"I mean it!" Dave insisted. "Look!"

He pulled a small brown box out of his jacket pocket. Digging his thumb into one end of it, he yanked a flap open and poured the contents into his palm. A spool of thin copper wire, insulated, preceded five tiny objects that looked like miniature bowls.

"Flash pots!" Dave said. "It's risky, but it's the only thing we've got!"

"I don't get it," A. J. said. "You gonna do a magic show for Keller while Sylvia and I slip out?"

"Yes," Dave said, to A. J.'s surprise. "Only I'll be slipping out with you! A. J., turn out the light for me!"

A. J. traded looks with Sylvia, who shrugged her shoulders. He went over and turned the light off while Dave dragged some boxes into position and stacked them. Then Dave climbed the boxes and tried to unscrew the light bulb.

"Ow!" he cried. "Too hot. Let's see—" He concentrated for a second, then tugged his T-shirt out of his pants and gripped the bulb with a fold of cloth. In a moment, the bulb was out. "Here, A. J.," Dave called. "Catch." He lobbed the bulb to A. J., who missed it. The bulb bounced off a box and shattered on the floor.

"No fair," A. J. complained. "I can't see."

Without the light, the gloom in the storage room masked Dave's activities. "Then that's even better," Dave said. "We won't need the light bulb anyway, if this goes right." He wound the copper wire onto the small contact points where the bulb had been. "It's after sunset," he said, after glancing out the window grill. "In another ten minutes it'll be dark. That's better still. A. J., would you create another one of your cardboard skyscrapers? Over there, beside the door."

Some of Dave's sudden enthusiasm began to infect the other two. They grabbed boxes and shuffled them around until a stack nearly ceiling high stood to the left of the door, near the light switch.

Dave clambered down from his stack and let out some of the copper line. One end firmly held in the socket where the light had been. He then used his teeth to strip away some of the insulation and wrapped the bare wire around contact points on one of the tiny bowls. When that bowl dangled from the wire, he let out more wire which he connected to the next bowl, and so on, until all five bowls hung from the wire, each about five feet from the other.

"Hold this, A. J.!" Dave said. He handed A. J. the wire,

then hopped up on the stack of boxes near the door. "Okay. Give it back now." As he leaned down, A. J. stretched up and passed the wire to him, and Dave wedged it beneath the top box in the pile. Now the wire looped from the light fixture to the stack of boxes beside the door, with two of the flash pots dangling at eye level. Most of the wire trailed from the stack of boxes to the floor.

"Another pile, you guys," Dave said. "On the right side of the door. But don't stack them so the door won't open."

All three of them worked in silence for several minutes. When the third stack was done, Dave ran the wire from the left stack to the right stack and back. A zigzag of wire connected the boxes, at eye-level, with the flash pots hanging in front of the door. He took the bare end of the wire and, with a couple of quick twists, attached it back to the top strand so that it made a complete circle.

Dave stood back and surveyed their work. His eyes followed the strand from the center of the ceiling, to the boxes, to the floor, and back to the ceiling. "Okay," he said at last. "I guess that's good enough."

"So what have we got?" Sylvia said. "I can barely see it."

"I'm not even sure what a flash pot is," said A. J.

"Magicians use them to vanish in a cloud of smoke," Dave explained. "The powder pots give off a sudden, brilliant flash. It's intense. Then they give out billows of smoke. While the audience is dazed by the flash, and while the smoke blocks their vision, the magician simply walks behind the curtain and no one sees how he left. Simple and effective."

"So the electricity in the wire must set them off," Sylvia realized. "All we have to do is flip the light switch and they'll all go off."

"Right. And one is all a magician needs to use. Five of them should blind Keller for a good thirty seconds. Sylvia, you wait by the light switch, and when I give the signal, flip it on."

"Wow!" A. J. exclaimed. "I get it! If he can't see us, he can't stop us. But how will we get past him?"

"Here's the whole plan," Dave said. "First, we have to sucker him down here and make him open the door. What I'm going to do is kick that generator into high gear. Not only should the noise draw him down here, but if anything was left on when this place closed, it'll start running again. That's gotta get him down here in a hurry."

"Okay," A. J. said. "Sounds good so far. Then what?"

"On my signal, Sylvia will fire the flash pots. Remember, *we have to have our eyes closed.* If we get blinded too, we lose our advantage. A. J., you'll be waiting between the boxes. Keep your face turned away from the flash pots. As soon as they go off, you've got to come flying out of the smoke and hit him with everything you've got."

A. J. gasped. "Hit him? The man who's never without a weapon?"

"Not *hit* him hit him. I mean a body block."

"I know what you mean, and I know I'm the best athlete here, but that's still asking a lot."

"Okay. You hit him low, and I'll hit him high. That gives us a weight advantage. He can't shoot what he can't see, and he might not have his gun out. And we'll have the element of surprise. A. J., it's the only way!"

A. J. looked doubtful. "That's awful risky. But I agree, there's nothing else to try."

"So maybe you can knock him over," Sylvia broke in. "Maybe he can't see for half a minute. We get out, but where do we go? He still has the gun!"

Dave scratched his head. "Well, that's kinda sticky, too. I don't know how much he'll be blinded. But my idea was to dodge into the Mirror Maze. I noticed when he walked us down here that the lock is off. Either he won't know we're in there, and we can slip out in the dark, or he'll follow us in there where he can't get a clear shot." Dave paused. "I think we can get through the maze faster than he can."

"But, Dave," A. J. said, "if he doesn't follow us in, won't he have us trapped?"

"Maybe not," Sylvia said. "I don't remember how the whole maze goes, but I remember that it exits on the other side of the building, on the back side of the rides you've seen. Behind Laff in the Dark and the Mirror Maze are bumper cars, and the spinning ride I told you about—The Whirlpool—and other things. He can't watch both sides at once. Dave, I think your idea might work!"

The three captives traded looks in the darkened room. The reality of the plan began to sink in. It had passed beyond speculation. They were going to do it.

"All right," Dave said. "You guys understand your part?"

"Wait," Sylvia said. "What about the flash pots themselves? How do we know they work?"

Dave gulped. "That's the worst part. I've never used them before; I've only read about them. I'm not sure if I hooked them up right or not."

"Can't we test one?" Sylvia asked.

"Not really. What if he sees the flash outside, or smoke gushing out the window?"

"We could just tell him we're planning a rock concert," A. J. offered.

No one knew what to say for a moment. "Okay," A. J. said. "So we're taking a chance. It's still worth a try, since they plan to kill us anyway, right?"

"That's a good point," Sylvia said. "If we die, I still want to die trying."

"And if we don't try, we know for sure we're dead," Dave said. "This has holes in it, but we have a chance. I think I'd better get things going before I have a chance to get any more frightened than I am now."

He turned and felt his way across the room to the other door. He pulled it open and suddenly realized another flaw in his plan. This second room had no window. He couldn't see the generator.

For a moment, Dave stared into the gloom, able to see only the dark outline of the machine. His mouth felt dry and adrenalin churned in his stomach. He was afraid the other two would see that he didn't know what to do and would change their mind about the escape plan. Blindly, he stretched out his hands.

His fingers felt their way past the belt housing meant to protect hands from the whirling belt. The machine vibrated under his hands, and he felt the grease coating the cold metal. He closed his eyes and tried to visualize how the generator had looked when he saw it hours ago.

Slowly, he moved his hands across the machine, tracing each nook and projection, trying not to trap his hand behind a moving part. After a moment he recognized a tube that had to be the gas line to the throttle, and he followed it back to a butterfly valve. He pushed one finger against the valve, and the machine revved with each push.

Then he remembered seeing a switch. Below the butterfly valve, he felt it. He clicked it to one side and the generator snarled like an irritated lion. Suddenly the engine noise swelled, expanded, engulfed him.

Dave backed out of the room. His ears protested the motor's assault. He closed the door and hurried to his position behind A. J., behind the stack of boxes.

"Remember, *keep your eyes closed,*" Dave urged.

"Listen," A. J. said.

Over the heavy putt of the engine, they heard sounds from outside. Somewhere a tape of calliope music played through the park's public address system, then suddenly shut down. A golden glow poured through the tiny window as the night lights sprang to life.

For a moment nothing else happened. Then they heard footsteps tread the stairs up to the door.

Keys jingled. They heard the lock pop open, and the door began to open. In a controlled voice Keller began a threat he cut off after the first word.

Keller blinked into the dark room. He had his gun drawn, pointed ahead, and he looked larger than Dave remembered. Dave saw the man's puzzled reaction frozen into the split-second just before it shifted into readiness. *This is it,* Dave thought, and clamped his eyes shut.

"NOW!" he shouted.

10

The Mirror Maze
and the Octopus

 Through his closed eyelids, Dave sensed a searing white light and heard the sizzle of powder burning. The acrid smell of smoke filled his nostrils.

Keller choked off a cry of surprise. Dave slapped A. J. on the back as a signal and opened his eyes.

Keller was standing in the doorway, both arms wrapped around his face. A. J. hurtled at him, fast and low, ducking the copper wires. Dave pushed against the floor with all his might and took three straining steps past the boxes. He leaped into the air, heading directly for Keller's chest, and tucked his head.

A. J. hit first in a rolling body block against the dazed man's legs. Keller lurched forward, off balance, just as Dave crashed into his chest, shoulder-first. For a moment all three seemed to be flying through the air as the impact knocked Keller backwards down the steps.

Suddenly a backbreaking jolt stopped them short as Keller's head and right shoulder hit the stairs, absorbing the force of the fall. Dimly Dave felt Sylvia scramble past them as he tried to untangle himself from Keller and A. J. Dave broke free, rolled down two more steps, and found his footing.

Moments later he found himself pounding into the night, mere feet behind A. J., dashing for the Mirror Maze. Dave gave one frightened glance back, and a fleet image burned into his brain. Keller, still spread across the steps, dazed, gripping his right shoulder with his left hand. The Luger on the ground, nearby, glinting in the moonlight. Dave wished he had seen it in time to grab it.

Then A. J. was throwing open the door to the maze. Light flooded onto the midway from inside, where Sylvia had already found the switch and rushed ahead. Dave paused just long enough to slam the door behind them, and they plunged into the maze.

Huge bulbs lined the panes of glass, like Hollywood make-up mirrors. Dave saw himself running toward himself, mouth open and panting, eyes wild. He dodged away from his reflection only to crash into a clear plate of glass. He bounced around it and threw himself further into the puzzle.

Three Sylvias seemed to be heading straight for him, then one; he realized she was in the alley next to his, separated only by sheets of glass. Three A. J.s appeared behind her. They ran along the short straightaway and vanished around another mirror.

Within seconds, Dave found the straightaway and ran along it. He strained to hear footsteps behind him or the slam of the door thrown open by the killer; but the thump and scrabble of Sylvia and A. J. rushing through the maze covered all other sounds.

Dave rounded another twist and saw Sylvia running at him from every direction. Suddenly the real Sylvia appeared before him.

"Oh, no!" she cried. "I ran in a circle!"

A shattering of glass announced A. J.'s presence ahead of them. "This way!" Dave yelped. "Left!"

A tortuous series of twists, and Dave saw, over Sylvia's shoulder, A. J. looking perplexed among a pocket of mirrors. Slash marks oozed slowly on his right arm, and a transparent sheet of glass lay in slivers at his feet.

For a moment, the reflections crowded them, staring back, exaggerating every move and expression a thousandfold. They were an endless mob, crushing in, surrounding the three with fear.

"Here!" Sylvia urged. "I remember now!" She rushed ahead, and the boys followed.

They fled into a network of distortion. Midget fugitives and panting giants flickered past. They seemed to run endlessly through trios of human ostriches pouring like syrup into stretch-faced wonders oozing into bubble-bellied freaks. When the exit finally swung into view, the pack of images mocked their relief in a spasm of wide-eyed mutations. They had entered a mirror-lined chamber. The exit, at the far end, had a mirror on it, too; but the red EXIT sign and the crash bar left no doubt. They slowed to a gasping walk.

"Whaddawedo," A. J. wheezed. "Goforit?"

"Listen," Sylvia said. A horde of monsters held its breath as the three strained to hear.

Deep in the heard of the maze, there was silence.

The army of stump-legged torsos exaled heavily and shifted its mass into a troop of floating heads. "He's not behind us," A. J. gulped. "Maybe he's out there." Several of A. J.'s heads jerked toward the exit.

"I don't," Dave puffed, "think so." He collapsed onto the floor. Some of the heads attached themselves to blobs of flesh and dropped with him. "When we hit the maze, he was still laying on the steps. I think maybe we injured him."

A. J. looked grim. "I sure hope so."

Dave panted some more and stared at A. J. "I know we hurt his shoulder. Maybe more. Maybe not."

"If I were Keller," the Sylvias said, "I wouldn't follow us into this maze. I'd go back to my gun collection and get a high-powered rifle with a night scope."

"And then follow us into the maze?" Dave asked.

"He hasn't followed us yet," Sylvia said. The logic seemed to click suddenly in her brain. "There's only one way off this island, and I'd go there with my rifle and wait for the prisoners to try and escape. And I'd happily wait just about forever because there's nowhere else they can go but the ticket booth. And if they don't come to me, when Dennis gets back, I'd go to them. And because the little brats caused me so much trouble, I'd take great pleasure in killing them." She shuddered with revulsion at her own words.

The midgets and the monsters and the malformations dropped their jaws and gaped. The Sylvias were right.

Dave dropped his head on his knees. "Oh, God," he said with his eyes closed. After a moment he looked at Sylvia and said, "Think, Sylvia. Don't we have any options?"

"Well—if we can't get to help, we have to get the help to come to us."

"Signal the mainland," Dave reflected. "If only we had a flare gun or something."

"Come on, you guys," A. J. pleaded. "Get up, Dave. We can't just sit here and talk. Let's go."

"We can't just go barging out there without a plan!" Sylvia countered. "We'll be killed."

"Then let's stay here," A. J. said. "Maybe he doesn't know where we went."

"We have to leave sometime," Dave said, standing. "And it's got to be before Dennis gets back."

Gravely, the crush of deformities stared at one another, hopeless.

"Think, think, think," Dave muttered. He reached up and scratched his head, and in response the mirrors made several flesh-snakes reach up and bite hairy points. "These mirrors are driving me *bats,*" Dave exploded. "Any other time this would be fun—"

He stopped.

"What's wrong?" A. J. said.

"The lights are on."

Sylvia snorted. "Well of course they are. You accelerated that generator, remember."

"Maybe the other rides work, too," Dave suggested.

It took a moment for the implication to sink in. Then Sylvia's eyes lit up. "I see." She thought another moment. "Yes, the place was working fine when they closed it. At most it's been two years."

A. J. caught on. "Ooohh. Not bad, Sherlock! Man, if you could get that Octopus going, someone would have to come check it out! Especially after two years!"

"Not even Keller could explain that very fast," Dave said.

"The Hammer," Sylvia said. "There's a ride at the west end of the roller coaster called the Hammer. It's at least forty feet high. There's an arm with capsules at each end where people ride, and the whole thing spins vertically—"

"I know what it is," Dave interrupted. "Does it light up?"

"Yes."

"Does the Octopus?"

"Yes."

"Ferris wheel?"

"Yes."

"All right. Maybe we're on to something. Here's my plan, then." A gaggle of hybrids leaned in to hear better. "Out the back door. If he's as smart as you say, he shouldn't be there; he'll be at the ticket booth. The Hammer is at the far end of the island. We'll sneak down there, and I'll try to start it while you guys keep a lookout."

"Wait," Sylvia said, "the most logical thing would be to

cover both our options. If the ride works, Keller will have to come running to shut it down. That means no one will be guarding the gate. It also means whoever starts the ride is likely to get caught or shot."

"So someone should sneak toward the ticket booth and slip out after the ride starts," Dave finished.

"That's risky, too," A. J. reminded them. "There's a wide-open stretch from the end of the midway to the ticket booths, remember? The only cover is a merry-go-round on one side and the Ferris wheel on the other. But they aren't close to the entrance. And then there's the parking lot and then there's the bridge, and if he's got a rifle—"

"If he stays there, we let the rides play until help comes," Dave said. "If they'll start."

"It's something to do," Sylvia began. Suddenly, far behind them, came a muffled thump. Dave's heart jumped into his throat.

"The door!" A. J. whispered.

Light, rapid footsteps sounded in the maze. Keller was winding his way toward them, quickly and efficiently.

"I thought you said he was smart!" A. J. hissed at Sylvia.

"I'm sorry, he's only right," Sylvia retorted.

Dave shuddered as he reached an inescapable conclusion. "Listen fast. I'm the most mechanical, and one can sneak better than two. I'll try to sucker him away from the gate with The Hammer. You two head for the ticket booth and do your best to get off this island. Let's go!"

Dave read the argument in A. J.'s face, but they both knew there was no time. Dave hit the crash bar and a thousand blobs and abominations fled into the park.

Dave glanced around quickly. The exit of the Mirror Maze presented an area as wide-open as the midway. Two football fields away, to his right, he saw the Hammer gleaming motionless against the stars. Straight ahead, and extending nearly all the way to the Hammer, the cross-supports of the roller coaster promised shadows and protection. Dave darted for them.

As Dave hit the chain-link fence that protected the ride, he risked a backward glance. A. J., holding Sylvia's hand to drag her along, charged to the left, toward the main entrance. Quickly as possible, Dave half-climbed, half-vaulted the fence and hid behind a massive support, where he held his breath and watched the exit to the Mirror Maze.

He had hit the door so hard that it had wedged open. A rectangle of light projected onto the asphalt, and he could see into almost all of the final chamber. The mirrors, empty, waited.

He waited for his eyes to grow accustomed to the dark. Behind him, far away, he saw the great black bulk of the ocean, stretching to the horizon. To his left, the repeating Xs of countless cross-braces, interwoven with humps of track. To his right, the front of the park, A. J. and Sylvia already vanished. He eyed the bumper car ride next to the Mirror Maze and wondered if they had dived into cars for shelter.

Two shots sounded from inside the maze, deep and throaty compared to the Luger. At once Dave heard a shattering of glass, and the lights in the maze winked out. At first he thought something had spooked Keller and made him shoot. Then he realized that the professional had just shot a fuse box so that he couldn't be seen when he entered the last room.

High above, in the upper struts, the wind sighed. Dave shivered. Keller seemed a genius in his chosen field—all-powerful. Dave did not want to match wits with him.

He almost wished for the comparative safety of the storeroom prison; then a wave of anger blunted the fear. He wouldn't panic. They had gotten this far. Within the next two hours the outcome would probably be decided. *Lord, just two hours worth of guts,* Dave prayed.

Shadow against shadow, something moved in the Mirror Maze doorway. He strained to see across thirty dim feet.

There! One dull glint of moonlight across a moving rifle barrel. Dave's eyes burned as he forced them to see in the dark. Phosphenes spangled his vision, the after-image of the lighted room.

Then a sound, far to the right. Beyond the bumper cars the building ended in a clump of bushes. A bush had said. "Shh!"

Dave groaned inwardly. Apparently A. J. didn't know that "sss" carried through the air better than any other sound.

The rifle barrel gleamed once more, and the shadow disappeared.

Dave straightened. Which way had Keller gone? He strained to hear the crunch of a man's weight on asphalt or to see the dim form of the killer. After tense moments, he knew only one thing: he had lost his man. Which way had Keller gone? Had he heard A. J.? Had he seen Dave? Or neither?

Studying the path to his left, Dave exhaled softly. Perhaps he had better start toward his goal. If only he knew—

Come on, come on, Dave thought, pouring a bath of logic to quench his fears. The guy isn't superhuman. He can't know where I am, and he might not have heard that sound with the building in the way. He probably stepped back into the maze, waiting for us to give ourselves away; he knows we couldn't have gone very far. If I'm careful, he'll never guess where I am.

Dave studied the ground, making sure he wouldn't trip over something in the shadows. Then another thought caused him to break into a sweat. I've heard of night scopes. I wonder if he has one and if he can look through it and see like daytime.

For several minutes Dave clung to his support, feeling very naked and very afraid.

He stared through the forest of supports and braces toward the Hammer, which he couldn't even see from this vantage point, as though he could will it to light up and spin. Finally he fought down the fear, concluding that if the whole plan had begun in the daytime, he would still be trying to sneak along the props and buttresses. If he could get into the heart of them, they would make good cover even in daylight.

Dave scrutinized the Mirror Maze exit a final time. Was Keller just inside the shadows, waiting for movement to betray their position? Or was he on his way to the ticket booth, staking a hide-out right where they wanted him to? Dave couldn't tell. He held his breath and slid along an angled support, half expecting a bullet to end his hopes at any moment.

Another vertical brace provided shelter for him. Well, ten feet closer to the Hammer and still living, Dave thought. He peered out into the park again. Nothing moved.

Sinking to the ground, he submerged himself in the pool of shadows. He suddenly felt an overpowering urge to put the whole roller coaster between him and Keller's rifle, and he began to belly-crawl toward the sea. Until he finally slid under a hump of track, he felt as vulnerable as if he were crawling down the center of the midway, feeling Keller's eyes watching him the whole time.

Dave could barely fit underneath the track. That was good; that was protection. He slithered along underneath it, asphalt biting his elbows even through his sleeves, until the track lifted and curved into the sky. Then he resumed worming his way toward the ocean, working his way around the buttresses that blocked his path. Each additional support he put between him and the park meant another tiny measure of safety.

Long moments later he reached the far side of the roller coaster. On hands and knees in the dark, his left hand slid over the asphalt into nothingness. Caught off guard, he collapsed, his chin slamming the ground and his eyes staring down at the knife-edge drop to the sea. Loosened pebbles tumbled out into space, landing so far below that Dave couldn't even hear the splash. He lay in frozen panic at what had almost happened to him. Keller had told the truth. There were only two ways off the island.

Carefully, he inched backward until he felt his vertigo pass. Then, among the forest of girders, he stood.

Struts and buttresses blocked his view of the Mirror Maze completely. It had been worth the effort.

Shaken, he began working his way toward the Hammer. He walked upright but lingered behind each pillar, keeping to his cover. Never in his life had he concentrated so hard on trying to sneak.

As the minutes passed, alternating waves of boldness and terror seemed to wash over him. One moment he felt oh-so-clever at the logic of their daring plan that he darted more rapidly from brace to brace. The next moment he would hear a sound or glimpse moving shadows out of the corner of his eye and freeze in anguish. It seemed an eternity before he felt he had reached the halfway point.

Finally he had to stop and catch his breath. He jammed himself into a corner formed by an intersection of the scaffolding, well-hidden from the park, and inhaled deeply. He held the breath for a moment, then blew it out slowly. He gave his head a fierce shake. The tension had him quivering. Adrenalin pumped through his system as though his body were prepared to battle an entire army single-handed. He hoped intensely that his limbs wouldn't decide to have a Clumsy Attack right now.

High above, a sea breeze sprang up and wheezed through the tracks, building for a moment until his collar jumped up and glued itself to his cheek. When it died, the breeze left an eery silence in its wake.

Dave surveyed the distance ahead. He thought perhaps he could see the base of the Hammer through the maze of Xs. He remembered A. J. and Sylvia, waiting near the ticket booth for something to happen, and felt a surge of guilt as though he had been fooling around. He pushed off from the relative safety of the scaffolding and skulked on.

Minutes later he had threaded his way to a small shack set among the roller coaster's crutches. On the side the word "TATOOS" stood out in four-foot-high letters. To his right, a large opening in the pillars provided access to the rest of the park.

He darted to a vantage point behind the shack, where he decided to take the opportunity to see into the park. He had to know if Keller had followed him, waiting a clear shot. I'd rather be shot and get it over with than go through much more of this, he thought.

He peeked past the splintered wood of the shack, out toward the other rides. The bumper cars and Mirror Maze exit sat under shapeless shadows, far behind him. Somewhat closer, a shooting gallery squatted in silence, holding its darkness like a cloak around itself.

Nothing moved.

Directly across from the tatoo shack, another ride attracted Dave's attention. Square and boxy from the outside, it had two separate entrances. One stood open, and a single light burned within, revealing a rickety staircase that led up out of view. A faded painting covering the building portrayed mighty ships sinking into a violent whirlpool.

The light troubled him. Why was it on? Had it come on when he revved up the generator, sending electricity to outer limits of the park? Or had Keller been there and turned it on?

He tried to make his brain think like a professional killer's. What would be the advantage of leaving a light on? Let's see. Maybe some dumb jerk would spend so much time staring at it that I could sneak up behind him.

Dave whirled around. Had something moved, deep in the heart of the roller coaster? He couldn't tell.

He looked back at the light. Surely Keller was too smart to turn it on and go in there. Maybe . . . maybe he wants to distract me because he's hiding on the other side of the tatoo shack!

Dave nearly collapsed with fright. Now he didn't know which would prove more fatal—to move or stay.

Stop it, he ordered himself. Just stop it. You're torturing yourself with your head games. The light just happened to be left on and Keller must have headed for the front of the park. Stay with the plan. You're almost there.

Gathering his courage, Dave sidled along the back of the wooden building. Now he could definitely make out the base of the Hammer. He could also see the fifty open feet between the roller coaster and the ride.

All right, he thought. No one said it would be easy. Get going and get this over with.

Five minutes later he crouched his sweating body behind the chain-link fence that surrounded the Cyclone Racer and studied his next move. The Hammer hung motionless, as though painted against the starlight. Another fifty feet to the right the Octopus stood frozen in mid-contortion, its painted eyes staring at each other. Beyond and above, a skyway car swung feebly in the breeze.

Dave returned his attention to the Hammer. A waist-high fence surrounded it, providing a no-longer-needed buffer-zone for the arc of swinging cars. He spotted, at one point along the fence, the glass booth containing the controls. Somehow he would have to get inside that booth.

He fought an urge to turn back, to try and find Sylvia and A. J. and just flat-out run for it. Anything but this. Once the Hammer started, he had no idea how he would get away.

I prayed, Dave thought. Just reminding you, God. I need you now. Do something.

Dave stared in every direction, searching for the tinest motion, listening for the barest whisper of a noise, checking for Keller. The man could be anywhere, so he seemed to be everywhere. A moment of total stillness took away all excuse. He knew this was the moment.

He took a deep breath.

He leaped high against the fence and flung a leg over the top. For a moment his jeans snapped on the wire; then he fell to the pavement and landed running for the control booth.

He cleared the open area in seconds, racing in a crouch, circling until he reached the glass hut. At the door he fell to the ground and lay in a pool of shadows, listening for a reaction.

Nothing but his heart thudding like a timpani.

After a moment he rose to his knees and pulled on the door knob.

The booth was locked.

Dave stared incredulously at the knob. He wrenched it again, the metallic rattle seemed to echo through the entire island. Locked.

He sank to his hands and knees. Locked. Geez. What do I do? Break the glass? Or follow my instincts and take a quiet walk off the nearest cliff? The disappointment pummeled him like a physical opponent.

All right, all right, don't panic, he told himself. Think. What do I do? Check for an override system at the base of the tower? Nah, not likely. Think. Don't panic. Splendini cannot save the world, but he knows someone who can.

Someone who'd *better,* anyway.

Come on, come on, think. There's always another way. What I know about picking locks wouldn't cover a postage stamp. There must be something else.

After a moment Dave forced himself to admit defeat. But he had hit on his next step. He had to try the Octopus.

The prospect of another sprint across open ground didn't

seem quite so frightening now that he had pulled it off once. He steeled himself and dashed toward the low fence around the other ride.

He reached the fence and vaulted over it, hunkering down on the other side while he got his bearings. Next to him, tentacles suspended some of the cars a scant two feet from the ground. The doors on the cars hinged on the bottom so that they could swing down to the ground and form a step up into the car. Even in the dark, the hinges looked rusted. The cars across the ride from him, perhaps fifty feet away, hung in the sky as if poised to swoop down and attack.

Looking at the rotted condition of the ride, Dave wondered if it would work at all. His eyes searched for the lever that would make the ride go and finally spotted it right next to the giant octopus head, inside a second small fence that bordered a quiet center in the middle of whirling confusion.

He felt another nervous wave about Keller's whereabouts. He gazed intently up the midway, searching for a sign of movement. All seemed still, except an occasional movement above where the breeze would push on a skyway car.

Dave picked his way into the heart of the tentacles, ducking some and stepping over others. He hopped over the inner fence and crouched next to the giant lever that started the ride.

A bewildering mishmash of gears and belts met his gaze. A nearby control panel held two toggle switches with lights above them to show when they were on. He reached up, flicked one of the switches, and heard a sputtering and a faint buzz. Bulbs lining the tentacles began to flicker on. Quickly, he shut the lights off. He had to get the ride in motion before he let it be seen. Another wave of paralyzing fear washed over him and he shook it off. Keller could have spotted the flickering lights; he had to hurry.

He pushed the other switch. Nothing happened, and the light above the switch didn't turn on. Next he found a dial near the base of the huge lever, so he twisted it as far as it would turn.

An electrical hum filled the air. Suddenly the ride seemed alive and ready to move. With grim satisfaction, Dave pushed the huge lever, nearly to the ground.

The head of the Octopus gave a jerk. All the tentacles quivered back and forth at the jolt of motion, causing some of the cars to spin lazily. The head began to rotate slowly. Rusted gears squealed in protest, but the Octopus turned. In slow-motion the tentacles began their rise and fall; gradually, the cars began to spin. He flicked on the lights again and made ready to clear out before the arms started moving too fast for him to dodge.

Dave swung one leg over the low inner fence, straddle-style. Anxious, he waited for the cars to lift into the air so he could run underneath them. In his mind, he pictured Keller at the ticket booth, startled by the lights and snatching his rifle, pounding down the midway but too far off to capture his prey. *Come on! Lift! Let me outta here!*

Ever so slowly the whirling cars began to rise. He brought his second leg over the fence and crouched to run.

A thrill of terror hit him when the deadly voice came from behind.

"*Freeze!* Don't take another step!"

Dave whipped his head around. Straddling the short fence on the outer perimeter stood Keller, a bloody gash near his right temple, a rifle aimed directly at Dave's head.

11

Merely Murder

The Octopus turned its empty grin toward Dave and waggled its tentacles at increasing speed. Out in the harbor, an arriving ferry shattered the night with the roar of its horn. Startled gulls wheeled and cried. Still, no one knew it was the end of the world.

Dave waited for his dizziness to pass. He had never known such fear.

"Turn off the machine!" the killer ordered.

The cars began to spin faster. "No," Dave choked.

Anger smoldered in Keller's eyes. "Maybe you don't understand. If you don't, I'll kill you."

Dave tried to swallow and found his body had temporarily forgotten how. This no longer seemed real to him; he couldn't remember the issues or the answers. He just knew that A. J., Sylvia, maybe the fate of nations, depended on him.

"Keller," he said. He could hardly talk. His tiny little victory was rapidly fading away. "You're going to kill me anyway. Why should I do what you say?" He blinked back tears and tried to steel himself to resist. "I can't stop you from shooting. But I am the only hostage you've got now."

A tentacle wavered past, throwing light across Keller's face. The blood on one side of his head made him look hideous, deranged. A grimace of pain flickered briefly in his expression and the rifle barrel wilted the merest fraction of an inch. Instantly he brought it back up.

Dave stared at the man, trying to guess his thoughts. Keller had to know that even if he shot him, it would take long minutes to get to the controls and figure them out. Meanwhile the mainland could see, and perhaps police would come—and the escape van was already gone. Sylvia and A. J. could be running for help at this very moment.

With frightening calm, Keller challenged, "The parking lot is wide. I have enough time after I kill you to recapture the other two. And I can keep your death a secret while I continue to bargain. Your father won't know if you're alive or not. Shut down the machine and I may go easy on you. If you don't, death will be the most merciful thing you can expect. Maybe I'll blow off your leg and let you bleed for a while." He gave a pleasant smile at the thought.

The tentacles approached full speed now, and the cars on the end of each arm began to spin in complete circles, picking up momentum.

Dave wanted to speak, but he couldn't. He trembled. Mute, he shook his head. Unable to reason any longer, moving on emotion alone, he took a timid step sideways, away from Keller. All he wanted was to be somewhere else, anywhere else . . . away.

Keller cursed. The cars had lowered again and robbed him of a clear shot. For a moment he winced again, holding the rifle butt against his injured shoulder with great difficulty.

Dave began to back away, bending low, moving in the same

direction as the Octopus, so he could see the tentacles coming at him.

The cars began to soar over Keller's head. He brought his other leg over the short fence and stood in the creature's lair, just out of reach of its whirling arms. As the cars floated higher, Keller began his menacing advance toward Dave.

Dave tried to back up faster. He didn't dare to take his eyes off Keller; if he turned his back to run, Keller would blast him. The menace stalked closer and closer.

Suddenly Dave stepped on his own pant cuff and fell over backward. And as the ride achieved full velocity, the centrifugal force began to fling some of the car doors open.

Keller crouched. His cheek pressed the stock of the weapon and his eye was hidden by the scope.

Suddenly, as one of the cars whirled over his head, the door dropped open and smashed Keller in the shoulder. A scream of agony and the thunder of the rifle tore the air. The man flew sideways and the rifle soared into the night. It landed butt-first on the asphalt, then skittered to a stop in the middle of the danger area.

Dave's eyes widened. *The rifle*—!

On his belly, he began crawling for the weapon. It was closer to Keller, but the man still lay stunned, crumpled like a rag on the blacktop. A brilliant tentacle swooped down from the dark and Dave flattened himself on the ground. The limb cleared his head by inches.

Keller moved slightly. He seemed groggy. He started to sit up, then suddenly flattened himself on his stomach and looked for the rifle. He saw it and began dragging himself toward it.

The tentacles seemed to lift away from Dave. He rose to all fours and risked a rapid crawl toward the weapon. Before he had crossed ten feet, a swinging car door rushed for him. Again he dropped, barely out of danger.

The gears of the ride still squealed. The Octopus began

accelerating out of control. The cars whirled feverishly and the arms waved up and down in wild agitation. The Octopus looked as though it were fighting a giant, invisible foe.

Keller still slid toward the weapon. A car flashed down and the door scraped the ground, throwing sparks at his face. The orange flash illuminated a look of rage and agony.

Now ten feet remained between Dave and the rifle. The whirling lights sent shadows chasing in circles as he struggled to belly-crawl the last few feet. Keller was still closer to the gun than he was.

The creak of the ride grew louder. Without warning, a car shot down; the door hit the ground and tore off, spinning wildly across the blacktop. Dave froze in place. There was another sound. A sustained cracking, a tearing of rusted metal—

One of the cars ripped away from its tentacle and flew into the night, flipping over in the air. From the dark, moments later, came a loud crash.

Dave tried to roll over and see what was happening. A shower of sparks shot up from the motor, and the Octopus head seemed to quiver and rock on its moorings.

Dave glanced at Keller. The man had stretched his hand out, inches from the rifle.

"Keller! *Look out!*" Dave screamed. He threw his arm up and pointed above Keller's head. The killer rolled over on his back and threw his hands up to defend himself.

Dave scrabbled the last few feet and closed one hand around the rifle before Keller realized he had been tricked. Dave closed his eyes and threw his body toward the outer fence, rolling over and over. The tentacles flashed over him, even faster, in the throes of death.

Dizziness gripped Dave as he hit the fence. He tried to watch the cars and time his escape, but the searing tentacles only made him dizzier. One stolen glance back revealed Keller belly-crawling after him, the incarnation of revenge.

Dave rose to his knees, grabbed the fence, and slithered over the top. As he fell to the asphalt on the outside of the ride, two more cars tore loose from their sea-rusted bolts and spiraled into the night. With tremendous force, they smashed into the Dunk the Clown! booth and caved in the front wall.

Dave staggered to his feet, the rifle clutched against his chest. Finally he could do what he had wanted to do all night and all day. He ran.

Behind him, the ride let out a mechanical shriek as the tentacles howled through the air beyond the speed they were made for. The sound crested and, despite himself, Dave turned to look.

A fountain of sparks shot up again from the Octopus's head. Suddenly the entire assembly seemed to lift up a foot higher, the cars whirling so madly they seemed to draw the creature off the ground.

Just as Dave noticed Keller rolling for the outer fence, two tentacles collapsed with a crash. The rows of light bulbs shattered as the tentacles hit the ground, and the arms burst into flames. The furious speed caused the arms to scrape along the ground in a complete circle before they dragged to a stop. The straining motor screamed defiance; then it erupted in a massive explosion. The head blew to one side and threw the ends of the tentacles into the air while the cars smashed to the ground in brightness like daylight. Smoke belched upwards, hiding shimmering heat waves and the crash of the tentacles.

Dave flung himself to the ground on top of the rifle and covered the back of his head. Chunks of wood and metal rained around him, some pelting his back.

Then, just as suddenly, it was all over. The Octopus lay still, silent and dark. Its head grinned foolishly in the flickering light of flames smoldering along the tentacles.

Dave's ragged breath filled his ears. He leaped up and pelted toward the ticket booth, tearing down the midway like a cyclone. Rapid footsteps echoed and bounced between the storeroom prison and the pinball arcade, the Mirror Maze and the Ride to Mars. The Laff in the Dark fat lady raised her hand in shock at the explosion.

Ahead, the merry-go-round and the Ferris wheel bracketed the exit to the parking lot. In mute astonishment, Sylvia and A. J. stood in plain sight, gawking at the plume of flame behind him.

A. J. caught sight of Dave running with the rifle and began jumping up and down and laughing. "He did it!" A. J. shouted, turning toward Sylvia as if she couldn't see for herself. "Splendini did it!"

Dave panted his way up to them. He hated to stop even for a moment. "Let's get out of here," he gasped. "I never—I've never been so scared in all my life!"

Even Sylvia looked ecstatic. "You've even got the rifle!" she warbled. "How did you do it?"

"What did you do to that sucker?" A. J. enthused. "This is better than bringing a scalp!"

"He—he might be dead." Dave didn't even want to turn and look. Instead, his sober expression served to calm the other two. "It was all an accident. This whole place must be ready to collapse. Let's get out of here before Dennis gets back!"

The three turned and scrambled over the ticket turnstiles, into the parking lot. Automatic lights, powered by the generator, illuminated the twenty acres as brightly as sunshine. Small in the distance stood the chain-link gate, their last barrier.

For a moment they stood together, intimidated by the length of the distance that still kept them captive. Dave hefted the rifle, wondering if he should toss it aside. It was heavy and Keller was . . . well, who knew about Keller. He decided to hang onto it. "Come on, let's get started," he said and began jogging toward the gate.

A. J. and Sylvia tagged behind him for a moment, then A. J. caught up. "Someone had to see or hear that explosion, Dave," his friend said. "Maybe help is on the way."

"It's all industrial over there," Sylvia called from behind, and after a moment she had caught up, too. "Look across there. It's all dark. Maybe no one did see it."

"It doesn't matter," Dave said. His mind would no longer tolerate the existence of what-ifs and possiblys. He was doing what he wanted; he was running. He was doing all he could. "Just keep going."

The lot seemed to stretch out forever ahead of them. Flower beds and lampposts dotted it, but nothing else marked their progress. Dave felt strangely naked in the wide-open expanse. He wanted to run, but he wanted to run hiding. If Dennis came back, there would be no defense.

Except, of course, the rifle.

Eventually they had to slow their pace. Despite the remnants of fear that haunted them, they couldn't sprint for an entire mile or more. Dave's uneasiness seemed matched by A. J.'s increasing confidence. "We're gonna make it, Dave," A. J. burst out after they had jogged in silence for a few minutes. "I don't know why you seem so bummed. We're almost outta here!"

Dave didn't answer; he just kept pumping.

"What happened back there, Dave?" Sylvia asked. Her lanky limbs gobbled up space as easily as A. J.'s; she had no trouble pacing the boys. "Are you all right?"

"I thought I would die any second," Dave said. "It's hard to forget. I just want to get it all behind me." Suddenly Dave looked Sylvia in the eye. "He had me trapped. I was *trapped!* He nearly shot me when he got hit—" His voice faded out. He couldn't bear to remember.

"It's all right," Sylvia comforted him. "It's over now. We'll get help soon. Look, we're over halfway to the gate now."

The gate was much closer now, its twelve-foot height reflecting the brilliance of the lights. The bridge stretched away from it into thick darkness, the shore only detectable by the absence of water reflections.

By now they had slowed to a brisk walk. Sylvia, clothed only in her sleeveless cotton top and jeans, shivered with cold now and then. A. J., absurdly enough, still had on the blue baseball cap that had plunged him into danger. The sea breezes tugged at Dave's hair and sent a chill through him.

Sylvia tried to draw him into a discussion. "I've got a theory about the Compudat inside man. I think I know who it is."

"Oh, yeah?" A. J. said with interest.

"I have an idea, too," Dave admitted.

"You first," Sylvia said.

"Well, when we watched the heat test at Compudat, A. J. needed room to lift Timmy, so I turned sideways and found myself staring over at Warren Michaels—you know, the new security guy with the curly hair?"

"The one with the shirt," Sylvia said. "And what a shirt!"

"I kinda liked it," A. J. said. "Didn't you like having Snoopy on it?"

"He liked yours, too," Dave said. "Maybe you should organize a trade." He paused to breathe. "Anyhow, before the experiment had gotten very far along, he got this real shifty-eyed look and snuck out of the room. A minute later, the alarms were set off—by hand. And after everyone evacuated, he was never accounted for."

"Wow!" A. J. exclaimed. "That's right! Do you suppose he was trying to meet Keller to get the plans from him?"

"That's a good thought!" Dave agreed. "Except I messed it up by breaking into dad's office!"

"Interesting," Sylvia ventured.

"That's not all," Dave said. Far out on the highway, a car streaked by. They stopped and held their breaths, hoping the car would turn onto the bridge, but it passed into the night. They resumed their march. "That night, my dad took me to a magic shop to buy those flash pots. Somebody tried to tail us home. We noticed them, because one of their headlights was dimmer than the other, and got away. When the car passed our hiding place, I only caught a glimpse of the driver, but his hair looked like Warren Michaels'."

"That's gotta be it, then!" A. J. said. "He must have hired on just to get the plans, and he was following you hoping for a chance to look in your car for the briefcase. You know, there's something phony about that guy. It must be him, because who else could it be?"

"I'll tell you who else," Sylvia said. "Howard Ludlum."

"Howard?" Dave said.

"Humpty Dumpty?" A. J. said.

"That's right. And I think the evidence is more convincing than the case against Warren Michaels."

"What evidence?" Dave urged. "Come on!"

"Look at the way the whole thing is set up," Sylvia said. "We know professionals are working with the inside man. The inside man doesn't need to go sneaking around starting fire alarms because someone else is causing it; he can keep his existence secret by looking perfectly innocent when the trouble starts. He also needs to know how to run computers so he can authenticate any plans delivered to him. Ludlum fills both those qualifications. He needs to blend with the crowd, not be the flashy sort that calls attention to himself. Ludlum fits there, too.

"You've also forgotten something important about Warren Michaels. He told you he once was a detective and he's now a security guard and his goal is to be an FBI agent!"

"What!" Dave burst out. "When did he tell us that?"

Sylvia gave Dave a puzzled look. "Why—the day you met him, of course!"

"I don't remember anything like that!" A. J. said.

"Don't you remember?" Sylvia said. "You were walking through all the corridors with him on the way to the heat chamber. He told you all kinds of stories, but I only heard the last little bit because I wasn't walking with you."

Dave whistled. "I missed that one all the way. I remember him talking, but it was all so ego-centered that I tuned out after a while. You were even yawning, A. J."

"That's right," A. J. said. "Sylvia tuned in at the end because she didn't have to hear all the other boring stuff."

"I guess a security guard would have to go through a pretty stiff security clearance before being hired, too," Dave said. "I'd overlooked that."

"Besides," Sylvia continued, "Howard also was not immediately accounted for after that non-existent fire. He joined the group eventually, but he was lost—he said. I believe he had tried to rendezvous with Keller."

"That's right," Dave said. "I remember he was last, but, Sylvia—he's the one that backed me up in saying there was no fire!"

"Why shouldn't he?" Sylvia said. "He knew it would be found out anyway."

"So far you don't have any more on Ludlum than I do on Michaels, though," Dave said. "Anything else?"

"Here's the finale," Sylvia said. "After Ludlum joined the group, you asked him if he had seen an intruder during the fire alarm. You mentioned 'a little dude with a beard.'"

"Yeah, and he didn't recall anything," Dave said. "So?"

"But he did," Sylvia contradicted. "You hadn't mentioned it yet, but Ludlum filled in a missing detail. He said the man had a *dark blond* beard. How would he know that if he never saw the man?"

Dave stopped in his tracks. "That's right! He did say a dark blond beard! But the only way he could know that—"

"—was if he was working with Keller!" A. J. finished. "My gosh, it fits!"

"But it still looked like Warren following us Monday night," Dave said. "Could Ludlum and Michaels possibly be working together?"

"That's a new thought to me," Sylvia admitted. "Keep walking. I want to find a brain older and wiser than mine."

They had nearly reached the entrance gate. The architects of the park had wanted a feeling of welcome to greet the tourists, so the expanse of parking lot at the entrance had several flower beds with saplings, junipers, and other ground cover. Around the edge of the lot, guardrails protected the chain-link fence and kept cars from nudging over the edge.

"Finally," A. J. said with relief. "Over the fence, then on to the mainland. "It's about time!"

"Only two ways off the island," Dave observed. "I almost fell over the edge when I was sneaking along underneath the roller coaster. There may be two ways off, but one of them will kill you."

A. J., in the lead, reached out and grabbed the fence. He prepared to shove his foot into one of the wire diamonds and began climbing. "But the other way," he said, "is merely—"

Suddenly a chunk of pavement flew away from A. J.'s feet with an ear-splitting whistle. In the next moment, the sound of a gunshot drifted to them from deep in the parking lot.

Startled, the trio spun around. In the electric glare, Keller struggled across the distance, obviously hurting. As they watched, he lifted a hand gun and flame spit from it. A split-second later, a metal pole above A. J.'s head ricocheted the bullet into the dark.

A. J. yelled and they dived for cover—Sylvia behind the guardrail, A. J. behind the thick concrete base of one of the lampposts, and Dave on his stomach behind one of the flower beds, protected by the curb.

"The rifle, Dave!" Sylvia called from her position. "Shoot back!"

Dave pressed the butt firmly against his shoulder and put his eye to the scope. "I've never done this before!" he called back. "I don't think I could hit him. I'm not even sure I *want* to!"

"He doesn't know that!" A. J. replied. "Shoot!"

Keller squeezed off two more shots. Before the sound reached them, the bullets whistled over their heads.

"Why hasn't he hit us?" Sylvia said. "He hit that sea gull!"

"I can see him in the scope!" Dave said. Magnified, the image showed the right side of Keller's head caked with blood. He was gritting his teeth in pain against each step he took, but he still lurched along in a half-run. One arm wrapped around his stomach as though holding his ribs together. "I think he's hurt bad!" Dave reported. "He can hardly lift his arm!"

"So stop giving him a chance to get better, Dave," A. J. urged. "Shoot!"

Dave gulped. After all he'd been through, he still didn't think he could kill a man. I'll give him a warning shot, Dave thought.

At first the scope seemed to waver all over the place; then he propped his elbow on the curb and placed the barrel on his hand. With dreadful accuracy, the cross hairs pinpointed where the message of death would be sent. He tried lining them up at Keller's feet. He felt like an amateur assassin.

He had a dim recollection of a lecture he'd heard somewhere, maybe in person, maybe on television. The expert had emphasized that "you don't *pull* the trigger, you *squeeze* the trigger." He saw what it meant now. If you jerked the rifle, you missed the target. Ever so slowly, bracing against the impact, he squeezed the trigger.

The gun gave a resounding click.

"What are you waiting for?" A. J. demanded. "Shoot, before he shoots us! He's getting closer!"

"I already did!" Dave yelled. "It doesn't work! It's broken or something!"

"What do we do now?" Sylvia said. "We can't climb twelve feet of gate while he shoots at us! We'd be sitting ducks!"

"We can't run," Dave said. "Same problem!"

There was a moment of silence. "Like I was about to say," A. J. mumbled. "One way off the island will kill you. The other is merely murder."

12

Splendini Takes a Bow

 Acres away, Keller stumbled to a halt. He stood in one spot and wavered from side to side.

Dave pressed his eye against the scope again for a closer view. Pain distorted the man's face. His beard and some of his clothes looked singed, and his twisted face glistened with sweat. It looked as though his ribs and shoulder were broken. Suddenly Dave remembered the conversation he had overheard in the van and realized what drove the man: if they escaped, Keller would die.

"Someone had to see that explosion!" A. J. insisted. "Help must be coming!"

"Help for Keller, you mean," Sylvia said. "Dennis is due back any time now."

A. J. peeked from cover at the reeling killer. "Maybe he'll do us a favor and drop dead."

Dave still gazed through the scope. Keller had his eyes shut tightly in pain. As Dave watched, the eyes opened a slit and peered toward them.

"It's a trick!" Dave said. "He's not as bad off as he looks. He's trying to pull us out of cover."

After a moment Keller lurched toward them again.

"Somebody do something!" Sylvia squealed.

"I guess we'll have to bluff him, Dave," A. J. said. "Stand up with the rifle and order him to throw down his weapon."

"*You* stand up with the rifle! He's an expert! He probably knows it might be jammed!"

"He doesn't know for sure," A. J. pleaded. "What else can we do? Throw rocks?"

"If he gets any closer, we'll have to go over the side and take our chances in the water," Dave said. "If we don't get shot hopping the fence."

They were so close to the last barrier; they couldn't turn back now. There had to be something—

Overhead, the parking lot lights flickered and dimmed, then flared back to normal brightness.

A. J. stared up. "How did he do that?"

Dave looked skyward. The lights blinked and flashed again.

Keller had stopped in his tracks and was staring at the nearest lamp. Suddenly he turned and ran for his victims with renewed speed.

"It's not him," Dave realized. "The generator is running out of gas!"

The lights faded out completely. The entire island turned to velvet black.

"Quick!" Dave urged. "Over the fence, before he can see us!"

In the dark, he could just make out the shimmer of the gate. No lights gleamed for miles around, but watery moonlight filtered through the fence. Dave ran over to it, Sylvia and A. J. by his side, and threw the rifle as high as he could. It cleared the gate easily and clattered to the road on the other side. Before it had landed, Dave had begun climbing furiously.

A. J. cleared the top first and jumped, rolling as he hit the ground. In a flash he was on his feet and holding the rifle.

As Sylvia and Dave swung their legs over the top wire, a dim spurt of flame shot forth from deep in the darkness. A bullet tore through one of the chain-links as though it were paper, inches from Sylvia's knee.

Dave and Sylvia dropped to the ground, running. Ahead, A. J. grasped the rifle in one hand and galloped into darkness.

The shore seemed no closer, but the gate slowly dwindled behind them. Two more shots whistled past, this time far from the mark. Desperate now, Keller must be hoping for luck.

"Seven," Sylvia grunted through clenched teeth as she ran. For a second Dave didn't understand; then he got it. Smart girl! She had counted the shots. Maybe Keller would run out of bullets.

They kept sprinting, trailing A. J. by mere yards now. The roadway flashed past underneath their feet, but Dave felt like he was running in place. Ahead, the bridge stretched dimly on—narrow, flat, unending.

Another shot sounded from behind, this time with a metallic clang. Dave glanced back over his shoulder. Keller had just shot the lock off the gate and, in the moonlight, Dave heard more than saw the fence swing open.

"Eight," Sylvia managed.

"How-many-bullets-does-a—" Dave whooshed out in one breath.

"I don't know!"

Fear pushed the trio. Ahead lay help and protection; behind, hatred and death. They ran as hard as they could.

Headlights swept around a distant bend in Pacific Coast Highway. Another vehicle approached the bridge.

Ahead, A. J. leaped up and down as he ran, waving, screaming. Sylvia and Dave joined in. The headlights neared the bridge—and slowed down!

"They see us!" A. J. shouted "They're going to make the turn!"

Then suspicion touched Dave. No one could see that far in this darkness, and they couldn't hear three kids half a mile away.

The vehicle passed under a solitary street lamp at the bridge entrance, and a telephone repair van sped onto the bridge.

"It's Dennis!" A. J. cried.

"What do we do?" Sylvia called.

Dave slowed, staring at the approaching headlights. They looked exactly like the ones in his nightmare, where he had been run over and killed. His heart dropped to the bridge, flat.

"It's no use," Dave said. "We're trapped."

"We've got to hide somewhere," A. J. said. "Even if we have to hang from the side of the bridge!"

Dave scrambled with the others toward the side of the bridge, already knowing in the pit of his stomach what they would see when they looked over the side: sheer concrete buttresses and a gut-wrenching drop to the depths below.

The van raised its beams to bright. Caught in the light, the three stood out in stark color against the black night.

"He's seen us!" A. J. yelled. "Run for it!"

"Run where?" Dave shouted.

Panic and confusion mingled in A. J.'s face. Suddenly, in the harsh shadows of the headlights, A. J. clenched his jaw with resolve, lifted the rifle to his shoulder, and pointed toward the van. "Maybe this will make him think twice—" A. J. began.

Sylvia slapped the barrel toward the ground. "What are you trying to do?" she hollered. "He'll see that thing and shoot you on the spot—he knows you can't hit him in a moving van. You'd never get a chance to try your bluff."

"Well we've gotta do something!" A. J. slammed the rifle to the ground in rage and fear.

"There's nothing we can do now," Dave said, too quietly. He stared into the darkness, wondering why Keller had stopped shooting. "It's not up to us any longer. It never really was."

A. J. stared at Dave, dumbfounded. Sylvia snapped, "At least we could have a selection from the choir." Dave ignored her.

Screeching tires announced the van's arrival. The door burst open as the van stopped, and Dennis leaped to the pavement, an automatic handgun trained on them. His face looked stern but his eyes glinted fear.

"Hold it!" he barked. "What are you doing here? Where's Keller?"

No one spoke. After a moment, Dave lifted his hands. The expression on the gunman's face made him not want to take any chances.

A voice came from inside the van. "What's going on? They nearly escaped—"

"Shut up! I'll handle this." Dennis paused for a moment as if considering options. Then he commanded A. J., "Kick that rifle to me."

A. J. glared at him but obeyed. One toe sent the rifle tumbling up against Bronston's feet.

The big man tore his eyes away from them just long enough to glance at the weapon. "It's Keller's all right," he told the person in the van.

With renewed urgency, he brandished the handgun and demanded, "Where's Keller?"

"Right there," Sylvia said.

Keller tottered into the glow of the headlights. His breath rasped loudly, and fatigue had stolen his proud posture. Singed, torn, and bleeding, he limped up to the van and leaned against it. "Don't worry," he wheezed. "I would have had them."

Dennis gazed in horror at the man, then allowed himself one short cough of a laugh. "Right. They were right in the palm of your hand. Blazes, what did they *do* to you?"

Keller stared back, still catching his breath. The Luger, in one hand, drooped toward the ground, while the other arm gripped his ribs. He tried to muster authority. "Never mind," he said, straightening. "Did you get the plans?"

"I did about as well as you," Dennis replied. Frenzy edged his voice. "I met our genius, here, at Compudat," he said, jerking his head toward the van. "He ran the blueprints through the computers and they're fake." Keller cursed, but Bronston continued. "That's not all. Someone must've figured out we were there. A car followed me when we left, but I drove back toward Agoura and gave him the slip in the foothills. They're onto us." He surveyed Keller's condition. "Face it, Keller—this job is blown. We've got to bail out."

Keller exploded. "No! Not while we have hostages, it's not! We still have the upper hand!"

"The party's over, Keller, can't you see that?" Bronston demanded as the sea breeze pushed at him. "If we want to continue, we have to kill one of these kids! Otherwise the government will think we don't mean business!"

"Of course we kill!" Keller rasped. "Was there ever any doubt?"

"We can't get away with it—"

"We *will* get away with it! We have the hostages!"

The men glared at each other, each measuring the other's will.

On the far side of the van, the passenger door popped open. Someone slid out, but the vehicle blocked Dave's view. A figure padded around the front of the van and came up beside Keller.

Howard Ludlum.

Beads of sweat shone on the chubby man's forehead. His

eyes darted nervously from Bronston to Keller, then to the captives. "Please," he said, "let me out of this. You only paid me to tell you when the blueprints would be on Mr. Scott's desk. I can't be involved in a—killing. I never imagined this would get so far out of control."

Keller's gun hand reached up and wiped a smear of blood away from his eye. "You worm," he sneered. "You've already compromised top secret material. It's treason. That's just as bad as murder, so what do you care?"

Ludlum tried to pull himself up to his full height. "I'm not like you," he said. "My only crime is that I needed money."

Suddenly Keller's arm shot out and the gun cracked Ludlum on the temple. Humpty Dumpty crumpled to the ground.

"What are you doing?" Bronston rumbled.

"Another hostage," Keller said with satisfaction. "To replace the one we're about to kill. A hostage with a pretty fair knowledge of some defense secrets. Maybe we'll throw him into the bargain, along with the blueprints."

Bronston started to make a comment when the breeze carried a sound to them. The man froze, pistol still covering his captives, head cocked to one side. A dull thudding noise, sustained and repeated, wafted down to them. "Choppers!" Dennis said. "They're after us!"

"We still have a strong position," Keller said. "You tie up this criminal genius while I deal with the brats." Keller licked his lips and grinned. "One of them is no longer necessary."

Dave trembled. "They're closing in, Keller," he tried. "They'll have this bridge blocked in a matter of minutes."

"They can bring all the help they want," Keller stated. "They won't shoot while I have you." He glanced at Sylvia. "And you." He fixed his piercing eyes on A. J. "But I don't suppose any officials would particularly miss you." Keller raised his gun and pointed it at A. J.'s head.

"No!" A. J. gasped. He raised his voice to be heard over the swelling sound of the helicopters. "Don't!"

"Drop it, Keller!"

Cupping his weapon in both strong hands, Dennis trained it directly on Keller. His voice strained under the tension.

Surprise flooded the killer. "What are you—"

"I said, *drop it!*"

Pure hatred burned in Keller's eyes, but his gun clattered to the ground.

"Hands up!" Bronston insisted. Keller didn't move. *"Hands up!"*

Slowly, Keller lifted his hands toward his head, never taking his eyes off Bronston. Dave could see the beast inside lurking, ready, waiting for the slightest opportunity to spring.

Bronston's voice seemed softer now. The helicopters had swept into plain sight, two of them coming in low over the coast, twinkling in the night. He ignored them. "Kick the gun over to me, Keller. And don't try any of your professional tricks. I won't hesitate to blow your head off. You know I won't."

Dave held his breath, afraid to move, unsure of the man's intentions. Instinct told him that Keller would fight more fiercely than a trapped rat, but so far Bronston's words seemed to have the right effect.

A. J.'s foot nudged Dave's. Carefully, so as not to attract attention, Dave turned his head until he could see A. J. beside him. A. J. was looking at the mainland end of the bridge. A car with a dim left headlight had just rushed onto the road.

Dave caught his breath. Bronston, detecting the sound, risked a glance at the captives, then quickly looked behind him and saw the car. He returned his attention to Keller before half a second had passed.

"Now what?" Keller jeered. "What did you accomplish? We're all caught." The sound of sirens drifted to them from across the city, reinforcing Keller's words. "You've made your point. We won't kill the kids. Let's throw them in the van and get out of here while we can."

Bronston spat. "You're a filthy liar, Keller. I know what'll happen the moment I take this gun off you. You're a wolverine, but I finally caught you without a weapon. What kind of animal does that make you now?" He let the question hang in the air.

Bronston turned to Dave, A. J., and Sylvia. "I'm helping you," he stated flatly. "I expect you to help me." He spoke more rapidly as the car approached. "I can't explain all this, but there's someone I care very much for. She believes in me. I can't betray her trust any longer." As the car drew closer, he became more sure of his decision. "For better or worse, I've got to turn myself in. You be sure and tell them that I never hurt you. Keller's right, we could've gotten away, but I chose not to. You'd better help me."

Dave wanted to respond, but right then the red Mustang squealed to a halt behind the van. The driver's door swung wide and Warren Michaels lurched into cover behind it, brandishing a revolver.

Reacting instinctively at the sight of the gun, Bronston spun and squeezed off two shots. The car door absorbed the bullets.

Michael's gun roared a response. Bronston grunted, and a spot of blood appeared in his abdomen. The huge man toppled to the ground.

Cat-like, Keller scooped up his gun and pounced on Dave. Dave found himself spun in a half-circle and suddenly pain tore through his right arm as Keller forced it up Dave's back in an arm-lock. The barrel of the gun crushed against Dave's head and stayed. He had just become a human shield.

Keller yanked on his arm. Something started to pop in Dave's arm socket but held, just on the edge of snapping. Dave held perfectly still.

Splendini!

In his left ear, he heard Keller's laughter. "Now," the kidnapper shouted, "throw your weapon out!"

Warren Michaels' forehead and eyes peered over the car door, framed by the window. After a moment he obeyed.

Just then a pack of police cars sped onto the bridge, sirens blasting. They swept to a halt behind Michaels' car, the four sets of headlights adding extra radiance to the scene. Behind the lights, dimly seen, policemen emerged and crouched behind their cars. Keller held his position and let Dave's expression do the talking.

"Stay back!" Michaels yelled, waving them off. "He's got Scott's son!"

At the same time, the first helicopter thundered by overhead, its searchlight stabbing down at Keller and Dave.

Splendini finally had his white-hot spotlight.

The gun barrel bored into Dave's head. "Police! Forget the sweet talk!" Keller roared. "I don't even want to hear it! Give me transportation out of here or I'll kill Scott's son!"

A bullhorn sliced through the roar of the helicopter. "We have you completely surrounded. There is no way of escape. Give yourself up."

"You can't shoot me," Dave said to Keller. "If you do, you've lost your protection. They know that. Let me go!"

"Shut up!" Keller snapped. "You've got it wrong. I've got all the hostages I need." He raised his voice and addressed Sylvia and A. J. "Get into the back of the van! No funny business or you'll be killing your friend! *Move!*"

The helicopters blustered helplessly in place. The army of policemen waited. It was Keller's show.

Slowly, A. J. stepped between the killer and the rescuers, over Ludlum's limp form, and into the open van. After a moment Keller glared at Sylvia and she began to follow. As she reached the open door, she turned toward Warren Michaels and shouted, "He has a Luger! He's fired eight shots already!"

Then she jumped into the van as if fearing Keller's response.

Dave heard Keller swear again, with quiet fluency. Michaels, still crouched behind the car door, lifted his head.

"Is that true, Keller?" he called.

Keller commended Michaels to a place of eternal torment.

"If it is, that means you're out of ammo. Lugers only hold eight rounds." Fixing his gaze on the killer, Michaels began to rise to his feet.

"Don't be a fool!" Keller shouted. "I reloaded! Get back or this kid is dead!"

"I don't believe you, mister," Michaels said. For the briefest second, his gaze flickered to the ground, past them, then back to Keller. "Why don't you prove it by taking a shot at me?" He stepped out from behind the car door.

"You've got all the proof you need!" Keller said. "Clear those men out! Now! I'm leaving!" He began to push Dave toward the van.

Suddenly Michaels screamed, *"Look out behind you!"*

Keller laughed. "That's the oldest trick in the—"

Out of the corner of his eye, Dave caught a glimpse of something large moving up from the ground. Keller spun, then snatched the pistol away from Dave's head. Dave looked to the side just in time to see Bronston lunge toward Keller. At point-blank range, Keller fired the Luger into the big man's chest. The gun clicked once, empty, and then Bronston had his hands on Keller's throat.

With a strangling cry, Keller let go of Dave and threw his hands around the massive forearms. Dave hurled himself to the ground and dived under the van.

Dave saw their feet scuffling back and forth as they locked in combat. Suddenly Keller cried out in anguish and the Luger hit the ground, inches from Dave. Before Dave could grab it, Bronston let out a shuddering sob and collapsed to the blacktop.

Splendini!

Suddenly a tide of policemen surrounded the two men. Three of them spun Keller around and slammed him up against the van while one knelt to check Bronston's pulse.

Dave began to crawl out from under the back of the van, and strong arms hooked under his armpits and pulled him to his feet. As the policeman helped Dave steady himself, he said, "David Scott? Are you all right?" Dave nodded mutely and tore himself away. He had to know about Bronston.

Mere feet away, a policeman was pillowing Bronston's head on a folded jacket. "Is he—is he—" Dave began.

"Just unconscious," the officer answered. "He'll live if we get some help. He's losing blood fast."

The chopping sounds grew louder as one of the helicopters began to lower itself for a landing on the bridge. Sylvia and A. J. clambered out of the van and stood very close to Dave— their threesome huddle complete again. Meanwhile, police shackled Keller's hands behind his back and hustled him to a squad car. Keller refused to lift his gaze from the ground.

Brilliantly lit in the night, the helicopter settled softly to the bridge, fifty yards ahead of the van. The running lights threw a dazzling radiance over the scene as the blades whipped up flurries of sand from the road. Bending low, four men in suits hopped from the chopper. Three of them strode briskly into the activity; one of them, holding a machine gun, issued sharp commands.

"Call an ambulance. Call two ambulances," he barked. One of the suited men ran back toward the helicopter; another bent over Ludlum.

Warren Michaels approached the man who gave orders. "You can clean up if you like," he grinned. "The real business is over."

The man did not smile. "That was pretty stupid."

"I took the chance. The girl said he was out of ammo. I saw the big fellow stirring, and I had to keep the other guy distracted. Maybe this makes up for me following the wrong man in the beginning."

The man surveyed Michaels for a moment, then nodded his head once as if commending him. "You had one right idea. There was an inside man." He gestured toward Ludlum, still crumpled on the ground.

"How about an application?" Warren said.

A brief pause. "See me later."

A silver Porsche rushed to a halt near the red Mustang II. Two more men in suit coats stepped out. Michaels turned and saw them and chuckled. He shouted, "Not you again!" and hurried toward them.

Now the fourth man from the helicopter, a slender man with red hair, approached the teenagers. He said one word. "Sylvia."

Sylvia jerked her head up. "FATHER!" she yelled, and hurled herself into the man's arms. He hugged her tightly, and they both laughed and cried at the same time.

A. J. worked his mouth, saying something to Dave that the noise of the helicopter covered.

"What?" Dave tried. "To the—no, *tell* the—tell the Lord?" He looked at A. J., who nodded with excitement.

Alexis Jerome placed his mouth against Dave's ear. "Tell the Lord," he shouted, "He's got Himself another boy!"

Dave's face broke into an enormous grin. "When it gets quieter," he shouted, "you can tell Him yourself!"

A. J. laughed. Conversation nearly impossible, he waved his arm to indicate the whole scene, looked at Dave, and shook his head in amazement.

Mr. Carrington finally managed to peel Sylvia off himself for a moment. He tapped A. J. on the shoulder to get the attention of both boys, then crooked his finger in a beckoning motion. "Climb on board!" he yelled. "Your parents want to see you!"

Dave whooped with glee. "Come on, A. J.!" he screamed. "We're going for a ride!"

They hurried over to the copter, where the pilot still waited in his seat. Last to clamber in, Dave turned to shut the door and got one last look at the bridge.

The telephone van, the red Mustang, the silver Porsche, and the squad cars sprawled across the road as though parked by madmen. Bronston and Ludlum had been stretched out on their backs, their heads pillowed by folded jackets, each one closely attended. Policemen slammed the car door shut on Keller as an ambulance pulled onto the bridge. Suddenly the engine of the helicopter accelerated, and Dave hastily closed the door and fell back into the bucket seat.

His chest went on a quick visit to the pit of his stomach as the chopper leaped from the ground. The bridge fell away below them, and in seconds the cars and lights were pinpricks in the immense black ocean.

"Circle the island!" A. J. begged. "Just once! I want to say goodby forever to that prison!"

The pilot grinned and gracefully brought the craft around. They began a loop of the island, with the search beam scanning the different rides and landmarks—now all dead and dark.

Carrington, Sylvia, and A. J. had all crammed into the back. "Oh, daddy," Sylvia said, "where have you been? I've missed you so much!" She placed her head against his chest, still tearful.

"Well," her father said awkwardly, "I can't really say until later—"

"It's all right, dad, really it is," Sylvia begged. "Dave and A. J.—oh, this is A. J.—they already know about the hyperspace transmitter and the Gang of 53 and everything. You can talk. Why didn't you contact me and mom?"

Carrington gave his daughter a squeeze, obviously a combination of great affection and relief. "The government caught wind of this plot," he said. "They wouldn't let me contact anyone for fear of giving away my position. I've been working on peaceful ways of employing the energy transmitter, and the discoveries became quite crucial. The last three weeks I've been at Compudat, working only at night so that no one would know I was there."

"But the helicopters," Dave said. "The police and those other men in suits—"

"FBI," offered Carrington.

"How did you know where we were?" Dave asked. "You saved our lives!"

"All I did was follow Ludlum!" Carrington's angular but pleasant features couldn't resist a grin. "Since I work secretly at night, Ludlum didn't know I was there tonight when he brought the phony blueprints in for a computer check. I saw the plans flickering past on a remote screen in the room where I was working. I snuck a look into the surrounding rooms until I saw who was observing my top-secret material, then called security. We followed him at a great distance, and he led us right to you!"

"How's my dad?" Dave said. "My mom? Have you talked with them?"

"Yeah," A. J. said. "My folks too!"

"Let's just say they'll be mighty glad to see you." Carrington smiled and gave Sylvia another squeeze. "We've radioed ahead, and they'll meet us at Compudat. They know that you're all right."

Dave looked down just in time to see the search beam finger the broken Octopus. "Wow," the pilot said. "What happened there?"

"Splendini happened there," A. J. answered. "Splendini and the Lord."

The pilot just shook his head, then straightened the chopper out of its circle and took off across the bay.

"So it was Warren Michaels following you that night after all," Sylvia said to Dave from her father's embrace. "I saw the car with the weak headlight tonight. But I don't think he was trying to hurt you. He must've been investigating the case on his own, following the 'inside man' theory."

"And thinking the inside man was my dad, I guess!" Dave said. "He must've panicked when my dad tried to lose him. And that other car, the silver Porsche—it was following us the other night, too!"

"That's FBI," the pilot offered. "Field agents for the southern California area. They probably were assigned to protect you and your father."

Dave laughed. "Poor old Warren! They must've thought he was the villain of the piece!"

"He's a hero now," A. J. said.

The lights of Los Angeles appeared ahead and below. Dave stared in fascination. In the night, from this altitude, the city looked magical, jewel-like. The chopper banked and headed inland.

"I have a question," Sylvia said. "How did they prepare a whole set of false blueprints in such a short time? Ones good enough to fool a scientist?"

"I can answer some of that," her father said. "The first I heard of the kidnappings was from Dean Scott. He told me that someone named Steve had called him from up at Arrowhead Mountain, where you kids had been. Steve was calling from a forest ranger's tower to report the kidnapping and an accident with the church bus."

"The forest ranger must've heard the gunshots!" Dave exclaimed. "So they weren't stranded there too long, after all!"

"And Compudat had all that night and the next day to make phony plans," A. J. said. "Pretty sharp."

"But I want to know how *you* are," Carrington said. "I can't believe you kids are all right!"

"I'm hungry!" A. J. announced. "That's how I am!"

"We're fine, dad, honest," Sylvia said. "And I've got two new friends!" She reached out and grabbed A. J.'s hand and gave him and Dave a big smile.

"And I didn't have to lose my friend," Dave said. "I thought for sure I would."

"And I think I've found the best friend of all," A. J. said. "And I don't mean you, Klutzini, even though you helped."

"And," Sylvia concluded, "I must tell you, Dave, that you've given me a lot to think about. I've seen a lot in the last three days that I've never seen before."

"If I had a tail, I'd wag it," Dave said. "I can't believe how happy I am. And I can't wait to see my family!"

A. J. sighed. "Me too," he said. "Even my bratty baby sister." He made a face, and they all laughed.

"I don't have to tell you you've been through a lot," Carrington said. "We still have a good thirty minutes to go, so why don't you all sit back and rest. There'll be plenty of time for talk when we land at Compudat, and believe me, you'll get a hero's welcome."

Dave eased back, deep into the seat. He was tired. His head and neck still ached from the bus accident, and scratches covered his arms and legs. Hunger gnawed at his insides. But he couldn't keep from smiling, inside and out.

Strange, he thought. The things that worried me so much a few days ago seem tiny now. Pimples and vocal chords and people's opinions of me aren't what life is made of; I shouldn't have had to go through all this to figure that out. You have to be yourself and let God handle the rest.

The minutes passed, and the engine drone became a lullaby of monotony. Dave wanted to taste every delicious moment, but found himself getting drowsier. After all the hours of plotting and running and fighting, he finally had his rest up in the night sky. . . .

Splendini!

The applause faded as Splendini motioned for silence, bathed in the white-hot spotlight. Resplendent in black top hat and tails, he waved a white-gloved but empty hand at the audience. He made the hand into a fist, gestured over it with the other hand, and then pulled a silver silk out of nowhere. The audience murmured.

Then Splendini crumpled the silk into a ball and hurled it from the stage. In midair, a flash of light changed the silk into a dove. The dove soared over the vast audience, then returned to rest on Splendini's shoulder as wave after wave of applause washed over him.

"Thank you!" his amplified voice boomed. "Thank you!"

The Great Splendini placed the white bird on its rainbow throne, but the applause wouldn't quit. In fact, the audience began cheering.

But Splendini no longer received the applause. Instead, he faced the dove, removed his top hat, and humbly bowed.